Neon Hearts

New City Series

Stefanie Simpson

Published by Stefanie Simpson

For us. For you and me. For surviving.
Disabled people deserve a happy ever after.

Books by the author

NEW CITY SERIES
A Goodnight's Sleep
The Way Home
Saving Suzy
Getting a Life
No Cure Required
Restoration Love

A NEW CITY STORY
Mutual Beginnings
Victoria Undone
Prelude to Hope
My Keeper
Best Friends Anthology
Love and Pretence
Chasing Elliot

OTHER WORKS
Demon Beauty
Witworth Doom Baby

ADVISORY: THIS BOOK CONTAINS MATURE CONTENT AND THEMES. Please visit stefaniesimpson.wordpress.com/books or scan the QR code for compiled content notes

Author's Note

This book is a disability centred romance. No one is magically cured, and I didn't create it as emotionally manipulative tragedy or as an inspirational meme. The abled gaze dictates many of the narratives around disabled people, and often our truths are erased by nondisabled people, dictating the terms of how disabled people are viewed. We rarely get to tell our stories on our terms. We're often told we cannot call ourselves disabled because it offends abled sensibilities. Others tell our stories with bias.

This is not that tale.

This book is about adjusting to disability. Accepting new realities and learning who we are in that. A question I've often asked myself is "who am I in this new brain?" One where time and memory are forever changed. When the words won't come, or my thinking is disjointed and chaotic. Without my memories, am I still me?

Yes, is the answer, even if that's a different version of me, I still exist. So this book, Bea's story and how she finds and accepts love, exists for me. The romance I needed when I became disabled. I hope, in a small way, this is that book for someone else. I hope it finds you, and you are loved.

Lemons

Bea steadied her breath, her heart beating hard and fast. Swallowing nausea, she closed her eyes and tensed as the MRI began in that small, enclosed space. A bubble of panic caught in her throat at the intense whirring noise surrounding her. Her fists clenched. How many had she had now?

CAPTA — the rehabilitation hospital where she was living — had been great. It'd saved her life, but she was restless and increasingly unhappy; frustrated at herself and the endless cycle of recovery, whatever that meant.

Instead of letting those thoughts consume her, she focused her mind on something else, keeping still as possible.

When her mum visited last month, she'd brought her a new phone. A window to the world. She still had to be cautious, and with new carefully curated SM accounts, Bea could move freely through the internet.

CAPTA had a FB group. It was a caring community with disability advocates — from whom Bea had learnt so much about her new life — it was positive, hopeful, yet honest and not patronising. There was no tragedy fodder or inspo porn. It was for people like Bea. Traumatic injury, recovery and adjustment.

She spent a lot of time in that private group and was making friends. Friends. It'd been an alien notion for a long time. She'd forgotten what that felt like. She'd lost all of hers and pretty much everything else.

Her earplugs didn't muffle the sound enough as her mind wandered. She centred her breathing as vertigo undid her stability, making her fall when she was still. A jolt of pain laced the inside of her skull. With a shuddering breath, tears filled her eyes, and she wanted to scream.

The juddering noise got louder, the space closed in, and she was in the car again. Trapped and cold. She shook wildly, and when her terror peaked, she held her breath, frozen.

"Hey." Freddy, one of her nurses, smiled down at her. It was over.

She couldn't stop shaking.

"Okay, you're okay." He soothed her. Bea was starting to realise she wasn't good with small spaces anymore.

Speech was impossible. Aside from a few sounds, she hadn't spoken since waking from her coma. Tears spilt down the side of her face, pooling in her hair, and that was the last thing she remembered.

Bea woke in her room, in bed, nestled in her pillows. The bed guards were up, and she had a foot through one of them. The sun was low, and everything was quiet.

There were times where she didn't remember — not that she wanted to — and those blissful quiet moments were respite. Then it all came back, usually nudging the back of her eyes with breath-stealing pain and blurry disorder.

Bea sat up and let the bed guard down as her head thumped and pain stabbed her eyeball. Slipping on her eye patch, the dark eased it.

Using her walker, she shuffled to the bathroom with her left leg dragging behind. She wore blue PJs covered with sloths, and her hair was bad. Wild dark curls stood on end. She lifted one side to show the growing out patch of shaved hair and the long scar there.

The stitches had gone, and she inspected it and then her face. It was strange not to know herself. Abstractly, she knew that the person in the

Time for therapy.

∞ ∞ ∞

"We were talking about your mum last session." Her therapist was kind. "But I see you're troubled today."

Their sessions were slow, but with the app, it'd be easier. She checked the privacy marker and typed her response. "I've been thinking about how I got here."

They'd not talked about her injury or why it happened or all the shitfuck decisions she made to get to that point.

"Do you want to talk about it?" Nadia seemed surprised.

"Yes and no," the artificial voice said.

"What do you want to say?"

Bea typed and deleted and typed again. "Guilt. I feel guilty for putting my mum in this position. That I was reckless and I wish I'd done it all differently."

"What exactly?"

"I should've quit. Left. Moved away. Not gone to the police. Not trusted anyone."

"Hindsight is wonderful. It can teach us how to go forward, but it's easy to stick at looking back. It's important you understand that you don't have to exist in your trauma and relive it, but you do need to treat it kindly and in a way that you can access.

"Sometimes we need to understand the past, so we can move on, even if that means only how we choose to think about it. You did the right thing. You saw something illegal and thought that people might be in danger; it's logical to try and put it right. It shows that you're a good person trying to do the right thing. It's all anyone can do. You are not the one at fault and didn't make a lot of those choices. They were made by others. These are the consequences of their actions. The only thing you can do is navigate your response to them. How you handle your recovery and new normal. How you think about the people that did this.

"That's the work you have to do. You cannot change their actions nor your own past actions. You can accept them. Learn from them if you need to. Do you have ideas about that?"

Bea typed and mistyped furiously. "I'm stronger than I knew. I'm still alive and grateful that I am." She paused and thought before carrying on. "Things that mattered to me before don't. I know what's important. I'm lonely. Afraid. I'm emotionally cut off."

"That's an understandable response. Sometimes when we shut down, it's a way of protecting ourselves. Our emotional vulnerability can be like a raw nerve, and your physical recovery has been a priority, which is natural. But now your body is healing, so you've got more emotional space to feel beyond the immediately physical."

Bea nodded. That was true. "Been having dreams and memories, but I don't know how much I can trust them."

"Memory is malleable. Would having clearer facts about what happened help you? Or is that something you're afraid of?"

"I want to know. It's annoying me." It was. The past mingled with nightmares, and so much was muddled. Her memory was often prompted by her mother, who'd become adept at bringing photos and telling stories.

"Let me prepare a session where we go through it."

Bea's eyes filled with tears, but she blinked them back.

"Have you cried yet?"

She shook her head. The mindset was power through, be strong and tough.

"You're allowed to. You're allowed to grieve for the pain and the trauma. You can mourn the changes and challenges. You don't have to love everything, but accepting it is important. You are not a tragedy, but that doesn't mean it's easy. It's painful and hard. Surviving what you did takes huge strength and resources. There's a cost to it. You must feel and process it. There's no quick answer. It will hurt, but it's worth it. Denying that truth will repress a lot of trauma, but you can only deal with it when you're ready to."

Bea hadn't cried or grieved. Not only the physical stuff, most of that were things she could deal with, but the fear lingered. The fucking terror that melted her brain for months, that was what she hadn't faced.

Part of her was worried she could never really deal with any of it.

The wall of it closed in. That breath on her neck again, hot and sickly, and she shuddered.

Bea cried. Ugly hoarse sobs wracked her body until her ribs hurt and her eyes were swollen. Nadia gave her a box of tissues and waited her out. The quiet nonjudgement was a relief. By the time she'd pulled herself together, their session was up.

"I'm going to structure something for our next session. Take some time to think of questions you have. Use your diary. Log your dreams and memories. Let the task form, sink in, rationalise. Decide how you want to think about it, how you feel about it. Okay?"

Bea typed. "Thank you."

Nadia smiled. "It's going to be all right."

Sometimes someone saying that is enough.

Bea ate lunch in the restaurant — they tried to make the cafeteria less like a cafeteria and it kind of worked — on her own. She didn't always want company. The low din was pleasant, but the light grated. She wore polarised sunglasses, and at least she didn't feel like a dick. People didn't care.

She picked at her food, head thumping. Setting her fork down, she scanned the room.

A table at one end had some of the employees there.

She spotted Ryan and a few other people she knew vaguely. Another was with them and had their back to her. Long dark blond hair, tight long-sleeved t-shirt, and a cap on. Odd to see that at a table.

Boredom and restlessness made Bea nosey, so she watched. Bea picked at her salad, feeling nauseated and left it, making her way back with her crutches, and thinking about the past.

Press

Josh Cotterill said his goodbyes to CAPTA first. He had so many mixed feelings about the place. It gave him a second chance to live but came with more pain than he could have ever comprehended.

Ryan shook his hand, and he said goodbye to everyone after lunch. Eight years had changed so much for him, and he wasn't the same person as he was then.

Turning from the beautiful grounds and hospital, he left. There was something that bothered him. He eased into his truck — an old pickup that served him well — and scowled, taking off his cap.

His long dirty blond hair streamed, and he tied it up into a bun for the drive over to Denbridge Security.

He checked his phone. He'd still moderate the group; it was important for him to feel connected to it. There she was. Bea didn't show her face, but there was a selfie of her in PJs with crutches in the garden. He smiled with the unscarred side of his face. The burn scars were patched with grafts on the lower right side of his face, neck, chest, back and down his thigh.

Josh didn't connect with people often, but something about her was sweet and vulnerable. Her posts always stood out to him. For a second, he wanted to go back and seek her out, just to say hi.

He stretched his jaw. No. For all his talk, he was a coward.

The drive into Chadford irritated him. The sprawl and traffic was everywhere, and he missed home. He knew he was doing the right thing. It was time.

Matt Denbridge was one of his few real friends. He was tall and imposing, yet he was gentle and grounded.

Mira, the office secretary and mother to all, stood up, rounded her impeccable desk and hugged him. Her curly black hair was peppered with grey, and he swore she was shrinking. "I'm very angry with you."

"I know. I deserve it." The one side of his face eased up into a smile.

She rubbed his back. "No. But anyway. Tea."

"Please."

Matt urged him into the meeting room. Selina joined them.

Sel was beautiful with short blond hair, and she was also utterly merciless. Neither of them lived in Chadford, and they shared one of the company flats when in town. She drank too much, had a filthy mouth and was forever trying to get him laid with someone she knew.

"Well, wonderboy." She flashed him a big grin.

"Fuck off." His voice was little more than a rasp after talking all morning with the people from CAPTA.

Matt was a wall of still calm, and he leant back in his chair.

"Listen up kids, Daddy's gonna speak."

He cut Selina a dry expression, his black eyes glittering and tanned golden skin glowing in the cold, low December sun streaming in. "Josh, I know you're here to resign."

Mira came in and set down drinks for everyone, and Selina opened some dockets. Josh's belly sank.

"I know what happened has shaken you, but we both know you've wanted out for a long time. Do you know what you'll do?"

Josh shifted. "ARC want a safety advisor in their domestic violence department. It's a distance gig, which works for me. I'll go through the process with people online who need to escape dangerous situations and help them organise. Liaise with police, security and that. I'll be in touch a lot. Plus, my family need help with their business."

"That's good." Matt glanced at Selina.

"There's one thing though," she said, her teasing gone and became all business.

"What?" Josh sipped his tea.

"There's a job which we think you'll be perfect for."

Matt leant forward. "It's the last job. Hand in your notice, do this job, make your annual bonus, and you're free and clear."

Josh sipped the honey and lemon. He loved that Mira knew what he liked. "I don't know. I failed you."

Matt looked his friend in the eye. "No. I know you take responsibility for what happened, but Willow is fine. It was all okay. I'm sorry you were attacked. I'm sorry for a lot of things."

"I don't know if I can do this again."

"We don't need you to do anything. Just sit and watch someone."

"Who?"

"A woman was nearly murdered. She's recovering but is a witness. The hired hand wasn't caught, but there's an ongoing investigation into something she saw and what happened to her."

"You're worried they'll finish the job?"

"Yes." Matt leant forward, elbows on the desk.

"She's in CAPTA. You're the perfect person to watch her." Selina's soft tone made Josh glance at her.

The floor opened up beneath him. "No. I can't put her at risk. I can't do it." A strange, unnerving buzzing in his mind interceded.

"Josh?" she asked.

He shook his head. The folder was right there, and he couldn't take it. The moment he saw the face, he'd be obliged. There was no way he could do it. None.

Matt put his hands up. "It's okay, I understand. Though let me make a suggestion. Think about counselling?"

The pain in his ribs eased, and where he could still sweat from grew wet and hot. Selina had a sad look on her face, and he felt humiliated. This had been who he was for years. A protector. Who was he when he couldn't do that?

Home

Josh went home. It was a long drive north to his sanctuary, and his mind switched off, focused on the road. Occasionally thoughts of Chadford and everything he left behind pushed into his mind.

He stopped for a coffee, the day growing bitter and dull, and dashed into the chain restaurant out of the cold.

A few people noticed him. His hair was down, the collar of his denim jacket turned up, and cap low.

He'd not shaved, and his scruff only grew on half his face. He absently scratched at it as he queued. The person behind the counter stared at him, unmoving after he made his order.

Josh pressed his lips together. "Is there a problem?" he ground out.

The young person blushed and focused on the till. "Eating in?"

"Not now." He paid and folded his arms, irritated. He fucking hated people. Reminding himself not to grind his teeth, he took a deep breath as he waited and scrolled his phone.

Bea posted about falling over in the garden. She used a laughing emoji, but his heart turned.

He commented, *aww no, hope you're okay.*

I'm all right! Just embarrassed but I'm gonna keep going.

Her profile photo was just her legs in cute PJs, and he didn't know why, but it made him smile. He wanted to message her. That might be creepy. He imagined she got all kinds of attention and didn't want to be That Guy.

As much as he wanted to assure her that he wasn't, there was no way he'd put that burden on her to navigate her response to him. It made him sad. It was so rare he was compelled to anyone, and the urge to reach out was huge. Not her problem, though. He didn't have many friends, and there were so few people he had any connection to. How could he explain that without being That Guy?

He shook off those thoughts without gaining any kind of answer and grabbed his food. Eating in the car, he let his thoughts turn over before replying to her.

Glad to hear it, you got this. You're doing great.

You're so kind, I really appreciate that x

He blushed, a kiss? She was just being nice.

Then he got a message notification. *I just wanted to say thank you for being so kind to me and supportive. This group has helped me so much, and you do a great job of keeping it positive. I've learnt a lot from what you've said. I don't have many friends anymore, and having this group really keeps me going.*

Josh debated his response for a second. *I'm glad it's helped you. It's hard adjusting, but CAPTA is a great place to be. I don't have many friends either, so I get it. I'm always here if you want to talk.*

She didn't reply. He finished his coffee and went home.

The narrow lanes were lined with thick hedgerows and bare trees. The hilly landscape of home took the tangled feeling in his belly away. Deerbank Lane wound higher with woodland at the bottom of the steep incline beyond the fencing, and away to the west was the valley that his cottage overlooked. The old oak that marked his potholed drive signalled the turning — hidden to most — and he eased along it. The garage was half-built. Building supplies filled one side of it. A skip and a pallet of bricks off to the side reminded him how much he had to do.

He rolled into the scant cover of the garage, and the emptiness of his life lay before him, but he shook it off with a sigh and grabbed his gear. The house was freezing.

Originally built in the 1800s, the ceilings were high enough for him, and Josh spent his time slowly restoring it. He'd done the kitchen, upstairs bathroom and the main bedroom and was working on the living room.

The kitchen spanned the back of the house, facing the woods and hills beyond wide patio doors. Terracotta tiles all through and a pale cornflower blue on the walls, and at one end he had a table and armchair where he sat reading most evenings, opposite the log burner.

He lit it, and then the range, making a cup of tea. When the kettle whistled, he took it without milk and carried it upstairs. The hall was freezing and missing half the floorboards. The stairs rounded an arched picture window with a deep seat, overlooking the wood, fields and village beyond.

His bedroom was frigid, and he clicked on the electric heater. He had solar panelling, so at least he had electricity. He wished he'd gotten the ground source and air pump heating installed in the summer and autumn. The ground was too frozen now to do it but come March, it'd be top on the list. Meanwhile, he could finish doing the inside.

He stood under the hot water of the walk-in shower. The black slate tile and glass suite were punctuated by a white sink and loo.

Oddly, he thought about Bea. What was it about her? Out of everyone who'd posted in the group over the years, why her?

Without any clarity, he shut off the powerful cascade of the rainfall shower and patted his skin dry. He had no mirror over the sink, shaved by feel, not really thinking of anything, and then massaged light emollient all over, including his face.

Dressed in sweats, he drank his tea and took a nap, still thinking about Bea.

When he woke, he absently checked his phone and found she'd messaged him back.

Actually, I would like to talk to someone. I'm in a bit of a tough spot with something, and I don't need advice, more that I want someone to know.

Every conceivable fear ran through his mind. *Are you in danger? Can I help you?*

Ugh, I'm sorry, I shouldn't have sent that message. I realised it when I sent it. I'm ok, please don't worry. It was a moment of panic.

You're safe with me. Tell me.

She didn't reply.

Into the Unknown

Josh knew. He'd thought about it in the silence of her not responding, and with sinking horror, he knew she was the Denbridge client.

He had his hair in a bun, gloves on and a fleece denim jacket. His breath puffed into the bitter morning air. He sniffed, the cold already numbing his face. He wandered down to the village through the narrow rambling path that skirted the woods and hurried to Sid and Edie's garage. They had the only petrol station and garage in the area without going to the big supermarket on the main byroad.

"How do." Edie dropped the 'h' and scowled at him from the chicken enclosure as she tried to urge the hens from the coop to collect the eggs.

"Where's Sid?" he called.

"In workshop. Where he always bloody is."

Josh smiled and shook his head. They weren't blood, but they'd raised and loved him.

Sid was 'retired' but still ran the garage.

"Here ye are." Sid didn't move from the oil check. "All settled?"

"Yes."

Sid stretched his back. He was a gentle but quiet man. He was fat with soft features and grey hair, and a deep voice that Josh never knew in anger. "There's a question in there." He peered over his glasses.

"Yeah, Pop." Josh couldn't call him dad — there was nothing good in the word — uncle never seemed right.

"A woman?"

Josh started tidying up.

"I see. We wondered..."

"What?"

"Well. You never brought anyone home, and we often thought perhaps you might be gay and were worried how we'd react. I know we're older but we're not old fashioned. Whatever makes you happy is fine with us because you're what matters. We love you as the child we never had."

Josh cleared his throat. His voice irritated him sometimes when it was very cold, and he waited for it to pass.

The garage smelt of oil and metal and the ever-present smell of petrol that defined his teens when they took him in as an angry homeless boy.

"No, not gay, but I'm..." he scratched his head. "Demisexual, I think."

"I don't know what that is." Sid wiped his hands, concern on his wrinkled face.

"It means I don't really experience... attraction for anyone much, I mean, I can, I just haven't really because I need to... care deeply about the person." He struggled to put it into words and fidgeted.

"Oh. I see. My brother were like that. Never had inclination for anyone. Back then, you didn't always know the whys of it. My mam asked him if he wanted to marry, he just said 'I'm not the marrying kind.' It were code for any number of things. Aye. Well, as long as you're happy in your life, that's all that matters to us." Sid sniffed and nodded.

Josh's throat burnt. "Thanks, Pop." He hugged the old man. His softness was a comfort as ever.

Sid patted his back. "Go and see Edie. She misses you."

Edie had Sunday dinner on and a cup of tea already set out. The kitchen was dated and cluttered, but the familiar comfort was that of home. She wore the same floral housecoat she always did. Her hair was short and peppered with white, and she was small. Her ill-fitting dentures whistled when she talked, and it belied the hardness of who she was. Yet under that, she was warm and generous.

"How'd it go?"

"I'm no longer employed."

"Have you decided what you're doing?" She pouted her mouth in concentration at peeling potatoes with her arthritic hands.

"Here." He took over.

"You're a good boy. I swear you're still growing."

"I'm going to help here more, do some distance work part-time."

"Sid'll love that. He can't keep up as much, and there's work to be had, people don't like going all the way up to bypass. And you know there's an estate being built."

"No."

"Oh aye, lots of work coming. Course, there's a lot of naysayers, but they're not local folk who need housing and jobs, bloody toffs."

Josh grinned with one side of his face. "Might get a dog."

"Ooh, lovely. I do miss having one. But Barbara..." She sucked her teeth. Barbara was the demon chicken of Deerbank, and she didn't take kindly to incursions onto her territory.

After Edie had fussed and cussed Sid for having oil on his hands — as if they hadn't had that conversation every day for more than forty years — they sat down for dinner.

Every now and again, he wondered about Bea. How she was, and the fear of what he'd left behind.

In the morning, still thinking about the apple crumble he ate and the leftovers Edie sent him home with, he checked his phone.

A few messages and a bunch of posts. He went through them after making coffee and cleaning and lighting the fire. He waited for the flame take through the glass and absently stroked a scar on his neck.

He opened the heavy curtains and saw a thick hoar frost over the hills, fog clinging to the ground. It'd be a cold one.

There was a message from Bea, and he was almost reluctant to open it. He scowled at it, heart thumping. He rang Matt.

"Well, miss us already?"

"Need to ask you something."

"Yeah?" Matt sounded like he was moving around in the office.

"Was the witness Beatrice?"

The sounds stilled. "First name terms, huh? Something I should know?"

"No. Just. She posts in the group I mod. She talks to me."

Matt was suspiciously quiet. "Well. Full of surprises. I can't discuss cases with you now. You know the rules. But I will say if you want to keep an eye on her, it might not be a bad idea."

Josh's heart ached.

"If it's any comfort to you, if you'd taken the job, it'd be a nightmare for boundaries."

Josh huffed a raspy agreement.

"Stay in touch."

"Thanks, man." He ended the call and scrubbed his face.

After a quick breakfast, mulling over her message and Matt, he got to work on the lounge. The plastering had been finished, he glued and tacked the skirting and put in the light switches and plug sockets. The big inglenook needed repointing, and he did that after lunch. It was a good day.

He messaged her back, finally deciding on his words.

I know who you are. I worked in personal security. I've left that job now and moving into a new phase of my life, but I know how this stuff works. I want to be here for you. If you are who I think you are, this will be hard, and you'll need someone who gets it and isn't close to it. I'd like to be that person if you want me to be.

Josh included his phone number. It was a risk, but he did it anyway.

Order

Bea stared at the message, reading and rereading until the words didn't make sense. Slipping her phone away, she focused on the daily living assessment.

Everything from using an oven to managing her money. Bea was a bit lost on most things.

She made a cup of tea, the two OTs making polite conversation with her.

She'd need some help when she left and became an outpatient. The anxiety of that happening churned in her. Bea did not want to live alone. She wanted her mum.

After her assessment, Bea declined yoga, she fucking hated it and went for a walk instead. The gardens were stark, and the day was cold, but it was nice to meander using her crutch. When cramp stole into her hip, she sat on a bench.

She kept thinking about the message from Josh and read it again.

"Everything all right?"

Bea jumped at the voice. Gina was a resident. About fifty, she used an electric wheelchair and parked up next to Bea. She had a thick coat on and a blanket over her legs. Her cheeks were pink with cold.

Though it was frosty, the sun was bright, and robins played on the bird table, hopping down from the tall evergreen trees. Bea snuggled into her big coat, breath puffing out into the air.

Gina shifted and smiled at the birds. "It's peaceful here. It's a good place."

Bea typed on her phone. "Rare."

Gina huffed a laugh. "I've been in a couple of places. One of them is the reason I was so ill. Still. At least they care here and actually want you to be well enough or have the things in place you need to go home."

Home. Bea couldn't go back to her hometown, not now. She wondered if she ever would. Or wanted to. Where was she going to go?

"You okay?"

Bea nestled her hands in her pockets with a death grip on her phone and nodded. Something caught her eye, and she leant forward and squinted. Movement beyond the trees. It appeared to be a man. Panic vibrated through her.

The figure went off.

Bea typed on her phone. "It's cold. We should head in." She checked all around.

"Okay." Gina furrowed her brow and made a turn.

They went in together, seeking tea and maybe cake, and Bea turned back once, just to check.

"Nina is off today." Freddy caught her attention in the large lounge they went into. "She apologises... are you all right?"

She'd hoped Nina would allay her fears in their session. Maybe it was anxiety over what they'd broach or Bea leaving. No, better safe than sorry because there were vulnerable people at CAPTA.

"I need to speak to my caseworker," she rasped out.

"Nina's just got a cold, she'll be back in a few days."

"No, not that. Important." Her voice went and squeaked, making her cough.

"Okay. Let me sort it out."

"What's going on?" Gina leant around a bit to face Bea.

her, they'd arrange care services. Bea relaxed. "I know I'm only there because of the risk."

"We can house you, put you under a new name. We can have Selina here be your escort for physio and that."

"Sounds expensive." She already owed Farooq so much, but he'd already started with the car insurance claim for her.

He smiled and raised a hand. "We work very closely with ARC. We've dealt with the funding. Your safety matters more. Plus, this is actually cheaper than CAPTA."

She huffed a laugh and agreed.

Acclimation

Selina wore a leather bomber, faded jeans and boots, and led her to her car. "Ready to pack up?"

Bea nodded sadly. She'd miss the place. It'd been a peaceful refuge through the worst time of her life, and they'd saved her.

She cringed, sitting in the car, and did every time now. On the drive over to CAPTA, Bea let herself remember waking for the first time:

In a snarl of uncertainty, a slow red awareness crept into Bea's consciousness. The backs of her eyes. Almost like she was looking down on herself, but not. Confused, she was small inside her body but realised that her body wouldn't move, and she swam inside it, unable to connect to her limbs.

The thought faded, and blackness took over. Psychedelic colour and pattern played in her vision, and it disappeared into red again, but this time she opened the red to white. Eyes, she opened her eyes. She was a thing, no, a person. The word person tripped through her mind, and she tried to say it, but only unfamiliar rasp came out.

Alien light and shape filled her vision, owls and trees, and strange monsters undulated and flexed, but when she blinked, they'd gone.

A face, she recognised that. Bea wanted to ask something but didn't know how; the words hovering but the texture unobtainable.

The sensation of being touched made her twitch. Painful and yet dulled. Noises and sounds lit up in her mind, and she winced, wanting to cower from them, sharp and angry, but she couldn't move.

Then everything went dark again.

"Bea?"

She opened her eyes, easier that time. She twitched and focused. Mum. She tried to smile but couldn't.

"It's okay, it's okay." She was crying and stroked the hair back from her face.

Bea didn't understand.

Movement flurried around her, and limp, she lay as things unfolded and warped around her. Sense returned to her fractured thoughts.

"It's over now, baby. It's all over with. You're safe."

Bea blinked and swallowed, finding it difficult. Jagged pain edged in, and it took her breath. More movement, and she floated off.

As sleep waited to take her, she remembered with absolute clarity what happened. The ringing nothing in her ears that followed, but she didn't have time to panic. The shock turned to white ringing.

Then she was dancing across fields, under stars, chased by some unseen terror, and those unfamiliar landscapes terrified her. There was nothing but that and a screech. All she wanted was the dark.

"Bea?" Sel asked.

Shaking, she shook off the tangled memory. Bea swallowed thickly, sweat clinging to her.

"It's okay."

Bea almost fell out of the car, hauling in cold and crisp air.

Using the crutch, she went in and to her room while Selina dealt with the paperwork.

Hospital was loud and uncomfortable, but less than two weeks after waking, she was transferred to CAPTA's high needs unit, and they helped her every step of the way. She wanted to say goodbye to everyone.

Freddy knocked on the door and came in. "I hear you're up and leaving us."

Bea burst into tears.

"Hey, it's okay." He put his arm around her, and Charles and Ryan came in.

"We just heard and escaped a meeting to see how you are." Ryan's concern set her off again.

"Bev has sessions but hopes you'll still come for appointments."

Bea gave a thumbs up, and Sel joined them.

"A party? Aww sweet. Let's go."

She stopped by and said goodbye to a few residents, sad she wouldn't get the leaving party that everyone had when they moved on from CAPTA.

The flat they took her to was small in a gated complex of several new blocks. Hers was little more than a studio, but it was enough. Bedroom. Small fold-out couch. A table and two chairs. Tiny separate kitchen and even smaller shower room.

"I know it's not much, but the building is very secure. You need a fob for the gate and front door." Selina passed it over. "Then, the code. These keys have to be securely cut at the brand's centre. There are lifts and on-site management. Here's the number." She added a business card to the fob. "Here is an emergency cord. This will alert Denbridge."

It was an orange pull chord in the bathroom.

"If you can get in this room, this door double bolts."

"Mum?" Bea rasped.

"Don't call her. We're contacting her, and she'll get in touch soon. Meantime, the internet should be on in a few hours. You'll need a food shop."

Everything was moving so quickly. After putting her things in the living room, they made a list and went to the giant supermarket on the ring road.

Bea bought everything she might need and a small leafy plant. Her first thought was to tell Josh about it all. Her heart skipped at the idea of talking to him again, even in the chaos.

Selina helped her put everything away. "Right. I need to do a few things."

"Thank you," the whisper of her voice was becoming normal to her.

"You're welcome. I have a fob and a key. I will not come unannounced unless it's an emergency. Anyone says they're Denbridge at that door without an appointment is lying."

"Right."

"Okay, I'm out. I'll be here tomorrow to take you to..." she checked through an app on her phone. "Hydrotherapy?"

"It's nice."

"Cool. Here's my number. You need anything, text me, I'm here for you. Will you be okay?" She put her number into Bea's phone.

Bea nodded. Sel gave Bea's shoulder a rub and left.

In the quiet of the tiny place, already dim as the grey day faded, Bea didn't know what to do with herself. She hadn't been alone for months. Gazing out over the grim cityscape, she wondered if this would be her home. Didn't feel like it. She put the TV on and made the bed in awkward slowness, taking breaks between tasks. With her things was an emergency bag. It had a stash of money, her paperwork and some essentials.

She slid it under the bed, the same place where she kept it at CAPTA. Bea wanted her mum. And Josh. She was tired, realising other than half a sandwich, she'd not eaten. She slowly made beans on toast, awkwardly trying to remember how to do it all, and sat with a mug of tea, curled up under the duvet.

Hey. I've had a hectic day, and I'm now in a flat eating beans on toast. She was pretty proud she managed it without dropping everything on the floor or burning the toast.

He replied, straight away. *Oh yeah? Nice?*

She took a selfie. Her hair was wildly curly, eyepatch on, her face drawn and tired, but she smiled, holding the plate of food. She was a mess and didn't really care.

She sent it with the monkey covering its eyes emoji.

You're beautiful.

Heat filled her face. *Not really. I'm a pirate.*

A beautiful pirate. He followed it immediately. *Sorry, I probably shouldn't have said that. I have no intention to be inappropriate, and if I am, I will totally back off.*

Bea blushed, her heart skipping. *It's been a long time since anyone called me beautiful. Thank you. It wasn't inappropriate. I'm drawn to you.*

You are? You don't know what I look like or anything about me.

Tell me.

The dots stopped and started while she ate.

35. White. Cis. Tall, I guess. I have long hair. Scars.

Bea took a moment, finishing her soggy, buttery toast, getting the bean sauce up. Those brief words felt difficult; something offered that wasn't usually freely given. That was precious. *Thank you. You've been lovely to me. Respectful and supportive. It's hard to explain how I feel. But I need to make a confession.*

Oh?

Bea was ashamed she knew about who he was. *I looked you up online. I needed to know if I could trust you. I'm sorry.*

He didn't answer right away, and Bea's heart squeezed as the dots appeared. *I see. I get why you would, and thank you for telling me.*

I understand if you don't think we should keep talking.

No. I really like talking to you.

Bea grinned. *Thank you. I've had a hard day, and I hurt now. I need to sleep.*

Of course. There are things I wish I could say.

Like what?

It'd be nice to hold you.

Her heart beat fast. She snuggled down, setting her plate aside. *Yeah? I'd like that. Feeling safe, falling asleep. Keeping warm.*

Sounds perfect. Goodnight x

Bea closed her eyes, nestling into the pillow, thinking of him. That indistinct figure holding tight and stroking her hair.

She hadn't slept so well since her coma.

Spark

Josh saved the photo. She was lovely. Tired with worry and fear in her face and no less beautiful for it. He had the impulse to take care of her. Fight to protect her and fall back into his past self. Even her confession, she hadn't needed to tell him that. It was touching.

That hair, though. He imagined holding her close and soothing those curls...

He shuddered a breath and stood up. No, it couldn't happen. This was dangerous, unlike him, and a bad idea. He'd gotten completely swept up for a minute, but that wasn't who he was. *It'd be nice to hold you.* Honest to fuck, what was he thinking. He'd never said the like to anyone. Yet the excitement fluttered in his belly, and he smiled. Maybe it would be okay.

He went to put another log on the fire but remembered he'd not brought the wood in. With a grunt, he went out to the store. The seasoned logs needed cutting, and the pile was low. He pulled on his gloves under the security light and set the first log, swinging the axe up and over, splintering the wood with a satisfying thump and crack. His mind cleared as he worked, breath misting into the night. When his arms ached, he stopped, wedging the axe into the stump where he cut and stretched his back.

Josh listened to a fox yip in the near distance and stared out over the hills. The hint of stars above him and the sprawling dark, open space centred him. He chucked the split logs into the basket, thinking about Bea. He let the idea of eating beans on toast with her under a duvet turn over.

It was a strange feeling. He'd never really connected with people like that. It unsettled him. The sense this would be dangerous filtered into his thoughts, but he shivered and headed into the warm.

He sat in his comfy chair, the low glow of fire flickering and clicked on the reading lamp. He had the urge to tell her so much, things he'd never really said aloud or barely thought.

For the first time, there was a hope of connection, and it frightened him. He needed advice.

He texted Matt, who rang him straight away, and he steeled himself for the piss-taking by adding more wood to the stove.

"Did you really ask me how to flirt?"

Josh flattened his mouth, recoiling at the heat from the log burner when the flame took. "I don't flirt. What is it? Is that what I'm doing?"

Matt laughed, rich and warm. "Just talk to her without expectation. Be considered and kind. Establish boundaries when you're not sure. Respect hers. That's it. Be honest."

Josh grunted. Matt was still laughing when he ended the call.

In the morning, he eased out of his warm bed, still dark out, and set up to decorate the lounge. He put on the radio and heater and sipped his third coffee.

His phone buzzed. *Morning x*

Morning. He snapped a photo of the room. *Guess what I'm doing today?*

Aww! It'll look fab, what colour? Such a beautiful space. I'm off to hydrotherapy today. She sent him a photo of her in her swimming costume.

He nearly dropped his cup. "Fucking hell." He cleared his throat.

You shouldn't send me photos like that.

You're right, I'm sorry.

It's okay, they're so intimate, and I can't reciprocate.

She didn't reply. He waited for her to respond, but no message came. "Shit."

Josh tried to focus but couldn't. He took a break after lining in. *Hey, I'm sorry I upset you. The photo you sent is gorgeous. This is weird for me because it's not something I do or have ever done. Talking to you is wonderful, and this feels precious, and I don't want to hurt you or take advantage.*

He kept staring at the photo. It wasn't explicit or leering but held soft warmth.

Later, his phone pinged as he sipped a tea, scowling at the patchy off-white walls, leaning back against the doorframe as the cold sun streamed in. It wasn't a big room but had corner windows and had slightly lower ceilings.

The rescue centre had approved him. Still with paint in his hair, he drove the five miles to the animal rescue centre, and the sound of barking dogs grew loud. He eased out, cap low and smoothly stalked through the busy wildlife sanctuary and to the rescue area.

In the small reception, a bright young person with turquoise hair beamed at him. "You're Josh, right?"

He cleared his throat with a nod.

The young person smiled. "Ready?"

Josh twitched a smile and followed them through. The kennel was noisy, and he wanted to take them all but settled on one to start with.

Bob. The dog was about two, a cross of who knew what, was the size of a car, had one ear, and a dopy grin. Bob had been in the kennel for eight months.

The tan and white dog snuffled the air as Josh approached, and then his back end took off wagging in a frenzy.

The ache in his heart lifted when he knelt on one knee. "Hey Bob, you want to come home?"

The dog dithered like a puppy, and as the gate swung open, he launched himself at Josh, vaulting up, and knocked him over.

Josh laughed as Bob licked his neck, and the two of them had a job of getting him up.

"He knows. You came back for him."

Blinking back emotion, he patted the dog, who was panting and wagging beyond excitement. Attaching the lead he bought, he led the excited dog out to his truck after signing the paperwork.

"Okay," Josh tugged his cap and opened the passenger door.

Expecting protest, he raised his brows in surprise as the dog jumped up and sat licking his lips and half-barked.

"All right then," Josh muttered, shutting the door.

The dog snuffled him, but when he started the car, he went quiet and still, occasionally barking at the trees as they passed them.

At home, he kept Bob on his lead, showing him the cottage. At least all the plastering was done and floorboards down.

Bob went straight to a bowl of water Josh had ready and messily lapped at it. Josh unclipped the lead, and Bob went to the patio windows by his armchair in the kitchen and lay down.

It was his spot. Josh grinned, but it faded as Bea's image sat next to Bob, stroking him played out. He closed his eyes. It was ridiculous. He didn't even know her, and she still hadn't messaged him back.

It was worth another go. *I hope you're okay. I have a new housemate.* Bob opened his mouth and panted so he appeared to be smiling when Josh snapped a pic. She didn't respond. She hadn't posted anything.

Sick worry knotted his gut.

I understand if you're upset, I get it. But please let me know you're okay. I'm worried.

His heart fluttered when she replied. *I'm fine. Love the dog. I'm so deeply sorry I sent that photo. I don't know why I did, I'm so embarrassed. It was wrong, and I apologise. I think it's best we don't talk anymore.*

Josh's throat burnt. *Please don't. My reaction wasn't what I meant. I feel a connection with you, and that's not something that happens easily for me. It scares me. You're so lovely and warm and funny, and I'm not sure what this means. I don't know what to do.*

Her reply was immediate. *Okay, I understand. It's hard for me to trust, and it's been so great to have that with you. I got carried away. I feel so awful, and I don't think we can keep talking. It's for the best, I'm sorry.*

Josh made an ugly noise. Bob whined in a yawn. Panic bit. He needed to put this right. *Can I call you?*

I can't speak much.

Please. I don't want to end this. An ugly sadness welled in him.

I don't know.

If this is it, then at least let's speak just once.

It took a few minutes for her to reply. *Okay.*

He sat in his chair and hit call, heart beating out of his chest. She answered after two rings.

"Hey," he croaked.

He heard the sharp intake of breath. "Hi." Her voice was quiet and small. It made him ache. She sniffed, and it sounded like she'd been crying.

"Bea. I'm sorry. It's hard to convey tone. I meant it warmly like you're killing me looking so good." He cleared his throat and sighed.

"It's okay. I'm so sorry." Her voice broke.

"Please, don't think about it again. I'm not offended or upset. It's a beautiful photo. You're beautiful."

She didn't answer.

"I picked the dog up today. Bob."

"Love him." She took a shaky breath.

Josh grinned. "Yeah?"

"Yeah."

"How was swimming?"

"Nice. Sandra, who helps me, is great. Feel like jelly. Relaxed." Her voice scraped.

"I know it's hard to talk."

"It is. Gotta practise."

"Bev?"

"Yeah." She laughed and coughed.

"Honey tea with lemon. Soothing."

"Thanks."

"Okay, I'll let you rest. Text you later?"

"Please."

Josh ended the call, thrilled and slumped back, grinning. Bob put his head on his knee.

"Let's show you your new home."

Rise

Bea grinned to herself. His voice was a gravelly rasp that went straight through her. Heat went between her legs.

She blinked, staring at the ceiling. The moment he spoke, her skin goosed. A litany of filth went through her mind in his voice. Was it wrong? Did it matter?

Nestling into the covers, she slipped her hand between her legs. It'd been so long. The indistinct image of him wrapped around her, lips on her skin, hands caressing her body, that raspy voice in her ear, needy and desperate. Dick inside her, other things, quiet ones that were for fantasy only.

Bea came hard and quick, the unexpected warmth of lust almost new to her. Her past lovers and boyfriends were casual. Sex was a sport, or it always had been. She didn't think that'd be open to her now, and the idea of hooking up didn't hold the thrill it once did.

Bea curled up, still embarrassed, but determined not to crowd him or be weird again. Or over-familiar. Yet she was compelled and comfortable with him. She imagined him behind her, spooning and pressing his face into her hair.

Bea shuffled to the door com in the morning, not quite awake. She pressed the button, and Sel's perky pixelated face beamed at her. "Thought you were supposed to text."

"I did. Got a gift."

Bea buzzed her in and opened the door. Behind her with a massive wheelie suitcase was her mum, Paula. The middle-aged woman had soft worry on her face and grey curly hair. Bea let out a sob, and her mother held her tight, swaying from side to side while she cried.

She soothed her child's hair, muttering quietly that it was okay.

"I'm going to take off."

Bea sniffed and hugged Selina, who just stood there.

"Be back at two tomorrow for therapy." She let the door click shut behind her.

Bea, watery-eyed and blotchy, stared at her mum.

"A very tall man brought me here and made sure I wasn't being watched. They're terribly paranoid but better safe than sorry."

"Work?"

"We should talk." Paula put the kettle on, tidying up as she went.

Bea fell onto the sofa, and her mum brought tea for them both. She'd missed her so much. Her smell and comfort. It'd been only them for so long. Bea missed their trips to the cinema and girls' nights where they'd do sheet masks and watch telly.

"I've been thinking, and just hear me out. I hate the distance and travelling. I bought my house a long time ago using that bit of money Uncle Nigel left me, and the mortgage is paid off. There's a lot of equity in it. Plus, work is offering voluntary redundancy packages. I've been there so long, I'd be better off taking the offer. I've already put in for it. House is on the market. It means I can be flexible for you. Be here to help you."

Bea started shaking her head.

"No, I want this. You need help, and there's nothing wrong with that. It's always been you and me." Paula cupped Bea's face. "I don't like my baby girl on her own and suffering."

Bea tensed so she wouldn't cry again.

"Now. Let's do something about your hair."

Bea laughed.

They were sat in a swanky hairdresser's with a coffee at lunch after Paula sweet-talked them into giving her an appointment and going through style magazines as they waited. The bright chatter distracted Bea, and she nearly didn't hear her mum.

"You never knew your nan. My mother. She had a stroke when I was thirteen."

"I didn't know that," she whispered.

"I had to take her care of her and your Uncle Nigel."

"I'm sorry."

Paula took a slow, steady breath, eyes fixed on the well-thumbed magazine. "It was hard. She couldn't speak or use the left side of her body. I washed her and cooked and kept the house. I wasn't alone, though, and we had help from neighbours and the like. Not a penny of money. Point is, we did what we had to, we adapted, and things were difficult, but she loved life. We'd laugh about things that'd happen, or she'd do. I cared for her until she died, and as hard as it was, it wasn't the end of the world. We just lived our lives."

Bea didn't know she was crying until Paula passed her a tissue.

"It's not going to be easy, but you're still you. Still beautiful and wild as you always were. Nothing less."

Bea closed her eyes, willing her emotion back.

"But your hair is a bird's nest. You and your bloody hair. Do you remember when you shaved your head?"

"No." Laughing through her tears, Bea blew her nose.

"You were six. A boy was giving you no end of grief about your hair. You came home from school and used your dad's clippers he'd left and cut it all off. The school had a fit. You had to wear a hat for three weeks." Paula rubbed Bea's back, and the hairdresser came over and ushered her to the sinks.

Bea had a conditioning treatment, and her long bob layered properly so curls hung full but artfully.

She might not be able to drive anymore. Or possibly work again, or remember ages eighteen to twenty-one, but she was still her. Spoke in a whisper and stuttered, forgetting words, and couldn't run or barely sing, but was still Bea.

"Lovely." Paula beamed at her.

When they got home, Paula cleaned a bit, and Bea went for a nap. She snapped a photo of her hair and nearly sent it to Josh but hesitated, not wanting to be embarrassed. She was ridiculous. They were friends, that's it. She needed to hold back.

∞ ∞ ∞

"You seem different."

Bea raised her eyebrows, shovelling a mouthful of stew in her mouth at dinner.

"Well, the last time I came up, you were... I don't know. Sad. There's a stillness to you that you never used to have. I assumed it was the injury, it's perfectly understandable."

"Now?"

"You're still subdued, but there's a bit of that light in you again. It's lovely."

Bea smiled before centring her breath to make her voice work. "Phone makes it easier. Support group. Friends." The blush crept up her neck as she stuttered.

Paula went still. "I see."

Bea sighed.

"Be careful."

"It's not..." she sipped her cooled honey tea. "He's sweet. No expectations. Friends."

"You like him, though?"

Bea nodded, suddenly fascinated by a carrot.

"Look, I'm not trying to dissuade you but are you sure he's safe? After everything that's happened, it seems prudent to be wary."

Her voice scratched, and she used her phone instead. "I know, and I have been. We're friends. He worked for Denbridge. He's a disability advocate, caring and gentle. Respects privacy."

"Good."

"If anything, he's warier. You don't need to worry."

"Worry is going to be my job for the rest of my life, dear."

Bea smiled. She loved the proper meals and fussing of her mum, who was pretty much her whole family. She was so relieved to have her back. Clearing her throat, she ate up.

She focused on washing up after dinner, leaning on a perching stool, trying to coordinate holding both the sponge and glass oven dish when her phone buzzed.

"That him?"

Bea scrubbed the oven dish harder.

"Why don't I finish up, and you go talk to him."

Bea huffed but kissed her cheek. Taking a cup of fresh tea, she gave her mum a dry glance and went to her room.

She felt bad that her mum had to stay on the fold-out settee, but it wasn't like Bea was an early riser or busy.

Hey you. She sipped her drink, waiting for a response, getting comfy in bed.

I was hoping I'd hear from you. Keep thinking about talking to you.

Me too. It was so lovely.

It was. How was your day?

Mum is here!! Got my hair done!

I'm so happy for you. Can I see?

Bea looked at the few photos she took and took another. She had a tee off one shoulder, lying back, hair pretty. Maybe it was too much, no matter, he asked for one.

Her heart fluttered when she sent it.

You're so beautiful. And your hair is so pretty. Can I call you, you know, to practise talking?

Please.

Josh's voice gave her butterflies. "It's beautiful, it must be nice to have it cut."

"Yes." She touched it. "I like it being played with." Heat rushed her face. Why had she said that? So much for restraint. She was cool once and took what she wanted without apology now? She was ridiculous.

He paused, and she heard his breath.

"Sorry. I didn't mean," she coughed. "I'm not-"

"No, I was just thinking about it. It looks so soft."

Bea didn't speak.

"Now I've embarrassed you."

"No." Bea laughed. "Is this weird?" She forced the pressure in her throat to gain volume and stuttered in the effort. "I used to have a good time. I haven't been that for so long. I'm different now. Yet you... I don't know what this is."

"Me either. But I'm curious to see where it goes."

"Yeah?" Bea curled up on her side.

"Yeah. So I'm going to think about wrapping a curl around my fingers."

Bea grinned. "I'll think about you doing that. I don't know what to picture." Her voice descended to a light whisper.

He hesitated. "Bea."

She waited, savouring the way he said her name.

"I was in a fire."

"I know. I'm here to listen if you need me."

"Thank you. I'm very scarred."

"Does it hurt?"

"Not anymore. I'll let you rest."

"Okay."

"Goodnight, Bea."

"Night."

She grinned into her pillow, feeling him behind her again. Head propped on hand, the other curling a lock of hair around his fingers. The sensation was comforting, and she closed her eyes. A bolt of sharp pain behind her eye shattered the moment, and she reached for the meds and drank her cool tea.

As they started to work, the floaty sensation crept up, and she floated with him, tangled up and safe.

A Truth

Bob licked his lips and watched as Josh laid the tile in the hall. Big limestone tiles. Josh worked until his back strained and ached from kneeling. The floor was half done.

He stretched up. Bob sat up and barked.

He slipped off his knee pads, put on his boots and thick checked hoodie coat, and clipped the lead on Bob's collar. He excitedly turned in circles, whining, his feet tapping on the tiles. They strolled out through the garden, Bob straining, snuffling everything, and at the end, they hopped the fence. Though the hills were green, everything held a stark emptiness of the countryside in winter. Tufts of dead plants mulching down under skeletal trees, and even the hedgerows seemed asleep. The bleakness seeped into him through the damp air. The ground was muddy, wet and half-frozen. He thought about Bea and telling her about his scars as they walked.

Josh had an odd relationship with them. In of themselves, he wasn't bothered. The associated trauma, however? He paused as Bob peed.

He should go back to therapy.

Bob was already covered in mud. It'd rained, leaving mushy puddles that he seemed to ferret out and enjoy. The dog was straining for a run, but Josh wasn't sure if he'd come when called yet. Too soon. He jogged with the dog beside him, and they travelled along the rambling path. Felt good to work out the tension in his back, and breathless, they slowed, approaching the village.

It was bigger than it used to be, but the centre was made up of grey stone houses and a small market cross, though there'd never been a market he knew of. The pub and shop-slash-community centre. A small children's park past the green. And Sid and Edie's garage.

He sniffed in the cold, his face numb and tight, and stretched it as he entered the yard.

"How do. Ya brought an horse." Edie laughed from the kitchen doorway, dropping the 'h' from horse.

Bob went on alert at the sight of chickens. Josh put him in the garden — divided from the coop — and Bob set watch on the feathery flock. Barbara, the demon chicken of Deerbank, clucked up to the fence. If there was ever a vicious, bitter dinosaur, it was Barbara. Josh was sure she'd peck Bob's eyes out given the chance.

Bob licked his lips.

"Come in, lad. It's too bloody cold," Edie called.

He reluctantly left the standoff, and his skin tingled in the warm of the kitchen.

"Here."

Edie passed him a tin of balm. It was plain and didn't smell good, but it soothed his skin. He sat with cake and a mug of tea.

"Anything need doing?" He patted on the salve.

"Aye. Always. Nowt that can't wait. Sid needs some help with a fence and gutters, but it's going to rain, and it's too cold."

"I'll come prepared in the morning. Spend the day. I'm in the middle of tiling." He blew on the cup.

"Having regrets?" Before he could answer, she called Sid in, and he came in with an awkward gait. Age was catching up to him, and Josh needed to step up a bit more.

"Well?" She asked while Sid cleaned up.

"No, I've done the right thing. I feel bad I've not been here for you more."

"Oh kid, don't be daft, you're young and need to live your life for you not us."

"You both did so much for me."

Edie bustled around for a minute, and Josh watched her. It was always the way when she was emotional. "You owe us nothing, and you gave us what we needed too. But I will say it's good to have you nearby, but you are not obligated. What's brought this on?" She sat back down.

"Nothing."

"Aye, I believe you." Her face said otherwise.

Sid returned and broke the moment, and Josh helped her serve a light lunch.

They weren't halfway through before there was an almighty to-do of squawking and barking.

Josh opened the door just as Barbara dashed past, and Bob followed. He ran after them both, managing to scoop up Barbara under his arm in an indignant kerfuffle as she circled him, flapping and pecking at his legs. Bob barked and jumped around, trying to get her. As Josh reached down, she squawked louder and attacked his arms furiously. She drew blood on his hand.

Edie stood in the doorway, laughing.

Josh pressed his lips together, marching to Edie, and she reached up and plucked a feather from his hair as Barbara strained to get revenge by pecking at anything she could reach.

"Best take the Shetland pony home. He's filthy."

Josh repressed a sigh and shoved Barbara with the other chickens before securing the coop's loose fence. She strutted off, the victor of battle by the way she went.

"I'll be back tomorrow." He waved after washing his hands and being supplied with a couple of plasters and trudged home with a sheepish Bob who stayed right by his side.

They went in via the utility and pantry off to the side of the kitchen. Next to that was the dining room that he'd not started yet, which doubled as a gym. He scowled at Bob, who gazed up at him with doleful eyes.

"Happy?"

The animal hung his head.

He could do with a downstairs washroom. Maybe he could put one in using part of the dining room. Josh stripped to his underwear, heaved up the animal who whined, and instantly covered him in mud.

"It's all right, you big baby." He kissed the top of the dog's head.

His body strained at the weight of the dog as he carried him upstairs. Josh locked the bathroom door and turned the water on after setting him down, showering them both off. Bob licked the shampoo off Josh as it went everywhere. The bathroom was soaked. He rubbed Bob down and opened the door, and he took off with the rips, drying off. He shook his head with a smile and finished showering.

Wrapped in his robe, he found the small mirror in the vanity unit and regarded himself. He barely ever did. In truth, it served as a reminder of the pain. Of the job that led to it. The mistakes he made. The hospital. Recovery. Fighting infection after infection. The soul-destroying itching that wouldn't sate.

He clenched his jaw. Maybe he should start looking at himself more. He wasn't ugly. He wasn't defined by his past, but it was part of who he was.

Feeling bold, he snapped a photo of himself, wet hair pushed over to one side, not quite facing the screen. The only thing that aesthetically bothered him was his partially missing ear. He shrugged his mouth down.

He took another with his face turned to the side so his scars wouldn't show as much. He zoomed in. He'd never really wanted anyone to think he was handsome before. It never bothered him. He deleted them so he wouldn't send them. He wasn't there yet.

What would Bea think? Still warm at their conversation, he couldn't resist sending her a message. *Hey. Thinking about you x*

He posted his daily message to the group, caught up on his notifications, and shared Bob's photo.

He didn't hear anything back from Bea.

∞ ∞ ∞

It was dark when he finished tiling and was hungry. Bob had zonked out by the log burner on a big beanie bed after his dinner and snored. Josh settled with a book and pasta, feeling uneasy about her when his phone pinged.

Can I talk to you? I don't want to put heavy stuff on you, but I think you'd understand.

He put his book down, heart in his feet. *You can tell me anything.*

She called him, already crying. He closed his eyes.

"It's okay."

She sniffed and croaked, but he couldn't understand her.

He sipped his drink. "I'm here. Imagine your head on my shoulder. I'm sat in my armchair. You curled up on me, my arms around you. Completely safe. It's quiet here. Dark. The log burner warming the room. Bob snoring."

"Sounds perfect," she whispered. Her breath hitched. "Therapy. Talked about what happened."

"It's hard. To face it. It never stops. You learn to compartmentalise it. Put it away. Make peace."

"Find a way through." She sounded drowsy.

The words itched on his tongue. He could help her. Be her way through. Josh stretched his face. "It'll be okay."

"Tell me something good."

He told her about the tiling and progress on the house. The fox he saw the other night. Bob and Barbara. He spoke until his voice was raw.

"Thank you," she slurred.

"Bea?"

"Pain meds."

"I'll say goodnight. I'd wrap a blanket around you, keeping you curled up on me."

She hummed.

"I'm blond."

He heard the smile in her voice. "Yeah?"

"I have it long. It's my only vanity."

She laughed.

Josh opened the folder of deleted photos not yet cleared, and he nearly sent one. Nearly.

Sex?

Bea's breath misted against the glass. Sleet fell steadily, and traffic crawled along the grey roads on a grey afternoon beyond in a grey city.

The police station was a sixties building with insipid everything.

DI Shah sat behind Bea with her large eyes intent on Bea's back.

The family interview suite was comfortable, but Bea had the feeling that she was in trouble and very unsafe.

Matt dominated the space, and he and Shah exchanged glances when they all entered, but Bea focused on the view of the city. Selina stayed close by, and Paula clutched a to-go cup. Farooq joined them. He was lanky, well dressed and every bit the solicitor. He had rich brown skin and curly black hair. They'd been thick as thieves as teens.

He'd come all the way to Chadford for this. He was introduced to everyone, and Bea repressed the urge to hug him and held her elbows instead when she faced the room.

He smirked at her.

Shah clicked her pen. "The Police Complaints Commission is moving forward with charges against Detective Abbot."

Bea forced herself to stay still. The man had been at the restaurant table when she overheard Micky. When she decided to go to the authorities, it was Abbot she spotted through the security glass heading for her in the police station. The ground had opened up beneath her at the realisation. It made sense for him to have a bent copper on his payroll.

Bea had bolted, and everything went to shit.

“I can’t go into much detail, but he is cooperating. That’s good. This is what we hoped would happen.”

Bea nodded and turned back to the window. Her eye screamed in pain, and she focused on it, pulling through her head and into her body.

“I know this is frustrating, but things are moving, and we’re in a good position. Obviously, I can make no guarantees.”

The others spoke about her, the possibility of a trial, the risks, but she didn’t join in. There was little she could do, and her say was limited. She had to let it unfold around her. Bea stretched her jaw and the electric nerve pulsed in her head.

She wished Josh was with her. She heard an ocean lapping and felt warm sand under her feet.

“Are you all right?” Sel leant in and offered her a mint.

Bea shrugged and popped the sweet in.

Farooq took her arm when they headed out of the room. “You look a lot better than the last time I saw you.”

“I was in a coma, right?” She offered a weak smile. “Thank you. For everything.” She gazed up into his eyes, willing him to understand what his help meant to her.

“Do you remember that time we got chased by that pack of year twelves, and you hid me in your room?”

Bea squeezed his arm. He'd been terrified, and they watched films and ate snacks until his older brother came and picked him up.

“Any time you need me, just let me know.” He hugged her before Sel hustled her away.

When they left, her head was pulsing louder. Sel and her mum helped her home and into bed. She took her meds with cold water and drifted off.

It was almost dark when she came to. Sluggish and weak, she used her new rollator with a seat to move about easier. No mum. Panic threaded through her, and she went to find her phone.

A text waited for her. *Just at the shop.*

Bea fetched a drink and relished the dim quiet. Not ten minutes later, Paula came back in laden with bags.

"We were out of everything, so I thought I'd let you rest. Feel better?"

Bea nodded.

"Thought I'd do sausage and mash." She started unpacking.

"Sounds nice."

"You all right?" Paula paused, holding the bottle of milk.

"What's going to happen? I didn't really take it in."

Her mum put the milk down and smoothed Bea's hair. "There's nothing we can do. We wait. We stay put. When the investigation moves forward, we'll know if you'll have to go to court. He'll go to prison."

Bea shuddered at the hot breath. "I hate it."

"I know. Won't be forever, poppet."

Bea smiled at the nickname.

Paula cupped Bea's cheek. "You're so pale. It'll be all right. Go back to bed."

Bea wasn't sure that was the case but kept her fear to herself.

That night, restless and anxious, she messaged Josh. *Hey.*

Hey you x I'm just reading in bed. His instant reply made her grin.

I need distracting.

Oh?

Big meeting today about what's going to happen. I'm afraid. Need something good.

So you messaged me?

Of course.

Am I distracting?

Very.

Her phone rang.

"How distracting am I?" His raspy voice made her shiver.

Bea laughed. "How long is your hair?"

He sighed. "Shoulders. Hang on."

A second later, a photo appeared. She couldn't believe it. Josh was turned away, hair cascading down, full and thick, over a cable jumper.

"Oh my god. Your hair is beautiful. And you're hot."

"You don't know that."

"Oh, I know that."

"Really?"

"Fuck, yes."

She heard his breath. "Bea."

The way he said it, gravelly and with a hint of need to the tone went straight between her legs. Swallowing, she clenched her thighs together. "You need to be careful about how you say my name."

"Why?"

"It's..." she laughed, the sound hoarse. "Hot."

"I should go." His tone sounded reluctant.

"Should you?"

"Yes."

With a hard breath, she forced out her faded, husky voice, stuttering as she did. "Okay. I'm going to think about how you say my name and imagine clutching your hair if that's okay."

"Very okay."

Bea grinned at the desperate tone of his voice.

Neither of them ended the call.

"Are you... will you..." She heard his swallow.

"What? Say it."

"I can't." He laughed. "Goodnight."

He ended the call.

She messaged him. *You're safe to say anything to me, you don't need to be embarrassed.*

Will you touch yourself?

Do you want me to?

Yes.

I am.

Thinking of me?

Always x

Two days passed, and she hadn't heard from him. Bea had come hard and fast thinking of Josh after their conversation, and she wondered if it'd gone too far. If she'd scared him or pushed too hard. She could agonise about that or her situation. He was better. Maybe. Her belly wasn't sure as it churned.

She had another session with Nadia. Therapy sucked arses sometimes.

They talked about their last session, her mum and Josh, and Bea was wrung out afterwards. She messaged him after reflecting on what they talked about.

Listen. If it was weird, I get it. If I pushed you too hard or you feel this is too much, please tell me. I don't want you to feel like you have to do anything.

That night, she had her reply. *I'm sorry for being silent. I've never done this before. I should've said I needed to think about it. Been trying to get a handle on how I feel and my reaction to you. You know I'm demi, right? This is new to me. I don't know what it is about you or me that's different.*

She was so relieved. *Oh I'm sorry, I didn't realise.*

Don't be. I'm processing.

Bea pressed her lips together to halt the burning emotion in her throat. Learning to navigate people all over again was hard, and she'd pushed him. Too keen. Too needy.

∞ ∞ ∞

Physical therapy was the most exciting thing on her calendar. Bea pushed the bar of the weights machine with her weaker side, and it pulled hard.

"Five more."

She shot Ryan a foul look.

Josh had messaged her regularly, and she replied. Their conversations were the highlight of her day as they unveiled themselves to each other, but she kept her distance and let him dictate the pace. She was careful about not sending him photos or pushing him sexually. Bea held back her wildness. He'd woken it up in her, and it was hard to temper. Getting harder and harder.

She stretched her legs out from the cramp. It would probably be best if she stopped talking to him before she did him any harm. The idea of doing anything to hurt him terrified her. Losing him scared her. Bea sank to the mat when she slipped off the machine.

"Hey, you okay?"

She nodded, and he helped her up.

"Okay, now sitting to stand."

Ryan observed and then made her do ten.

Every night for the past two weeks she'd touched herself, desperate for Josh's love. By the end of the session, she was on the verge of tears.

"Is the pain worse?" Ryan was full of concern.

Bea shook her head.

"Everything all right?"

"Fine."

He patted her shoulder.

Using her crutches, she made her way to the changing room. Bea was adrift.

She wanted to be who she'd been but couldn't. Finding out who she was now was out of reach somehow. It was cold, and she shivered.

Sel arrived just as Bea reached reception.

"You're quieter than usual," Sel said on the drive back to the flat.

Bea shrugged.

"Come on, we're friends."

"Don't know who I am now."

Sel scrunched her mouth to the side. "I know you're kind and sweet. Gentle, funny. You are who you are. If it's different now, then that's what it is, right? I like you."

"Thank you."

Later, in bed, he messaged her. *Is everything okay? You've been distant.*

The impulsive part of her would push, needy for him. Projecting onto him. *Everything is all right, I'm sorry.*

What's wrong?

Bea stared at the screen, trying to force herself to explain what she felt. What she wanted. She didn't.

Bea. Talk to me. You can say anything to me, please.

I think maybe we should step back from this. You've done nothing wrong. It's me. It's okay, I promise.

Why?

Because I'm the kind of person who sends photos to you unasked for. And googles you. Because I've pushed you. And I refuse to harm you. I want you and think you're the most wonderful person. So wonderful it makes my heart ache. I'm not good enough for you. I'm impulsive. Don't always think things through. She locked her phone and curled up, trying to resist reading the message he sent in reply. She couldn't resist.

I don't care. You've done nothing wrong and nothing to harm me. Josh's words echoed in his voice.

I'm sorry Josh. So sorry.

No.

No?

I really care about you. I love talking with you. I feel things with you I've never felt before. I want you.

Her heart pressed against her ribs. *I'm afraid.*

You're safe with me. I know I'm safe with you because you care. I want to hold you. Keep you safe and feel you near me. Know your smell and taste. I want to explore in ways that I've never really wanted or cared about. You bring something out in me.

Bea read it over and over again. *I want that. You make me bold.*

I like that.

He answered on the first ring.

"See, bold," she said, stuttering. "Which is the problem."

"It's not. I want it. I want you." He cleared his throat. "What would you do with me?"

Her face heated, and she licked her lips, her mind catching up. "Nothing strenuous. Maybe have you go down on me. Head between my legs, enjoying me. Making me come."

His breathing grew quicker.

"Climbing up between my legs, kissing me."

"How," he swallowed, "do you like oral?"

She hummed, nestling into the bed and sliding her free hand between her legs. "Hmm. Slow. Lots of tongue sliding over my clit. Two fingers massaging inside my pussy."

He made a rough but quiet growly noise.

She mimicked what she needed with her fingers. "Little soft kisses that make me shudder. Licks and soft sucks that make me squirm. Lazy and focused until I tremble and beg for more."

"Fuck, Bea."

"You want that?"

"Yes." He panted.

She kept touching herself, letting him hear her pleasure as she spiralled and came in breathless need, nerves and body tingling in heated bliss. Humming, she relaxed. "Josh?"

"Uh-huh."

"You with me?" Bea floated, embarrassed but hot for it.

It sounded like he was wanking. Bea bit her lip, floating and yet still desperate. "I want to hear you come. Imagine my hands on you, stroking you until-"

A strangled noise interrupted her, and silence sat between them for a minute.

"Oh my god," he moaned.

"Nice?"

"That was new. In a good way."

"It was. I need to sleep. Message me tomorrow."

"Promise."

Friends

Josh couldn't stop thinking about her. He fixed the fence in the howling, raw wind while Bob ran from one end of the enclosed pasture to the other.

He could almost feel her thighs around his head, and he hammered harder. This wasn't him. It wasn't. That connection was unexpected and brutal, and if he wasn't careful, it would consume him.

He finished and sipped coffee from his thermos. He couldn't feel his face, and even with work gloves, his hands were numb. He couldn't believe he got so carried away. She seemed to sweep him up and off somewhere else.

Bold. He made her bold. He smiled and watched the sheep grazing on the hillside in the distance.

He took a selfie. The winter sun was sharp and golden on his hair, and he looked good in his fleece-lined denim jacket. He did. His hair covered most of his face, Bob panting in the background, the countryside wintery but pretty on a clear, sharp day.

Bold.

He sent it.

Oh my god. I knew you were a hottie, but damn. You make me thirsty.

He laughed at all the emojis she included. *Shh.*

No. You're so gorgeous. Last night was the best.

It was amazing. I have some things I need to do, people I gotta deal with.

Okay xx

Part of him wanted to get in his car and go see her. The pull was sudden and urgent. He also wanted to find the people who were doing this and kill them. He could do it and fall into what he never wanted to be. The impulse was there with pressing darkness in his heart. He was never that reckless. He closed his eyes to it and then packed up. He washed up in the pink bathroom at Edie and Sid's.

"All done?" she asked.

"Yep." He took the tea Edie made him, and Bob fell asleep by the range.

"Off to town?"

"I am."

"What's up with you?"

He scowled.

"You've been more monosyllabic than usual."

He cut her a dry glance.

"Oh ah, I know big words, spill."

Josh cleared his throat and straightened the coaster. "I really like someone."

He thought Edie might choke on her dentures. "Well. I'm happy for you. Sid did mention what you told him. As long as you're happy."

"I..." He ran his hands through his hair.

"Oh lord, you got it bad."

"I might have."

Edie cackled as he sipped his tea. "Tell me about them."

"She's been through a lot. Gorgeous curly hair. Sweet. Funny. I think she's someone who just gets what it's like. The thing is, she's going through something, and I can't be there for her."

"Why?"

He took a minute and sipped. "It was a hard choice giving up Denbridge and the last connection to Chadford. Hard choice to make."

"And she'll put you right back in that place." Edie pursed her mouth. Her cheeks were red with spider veins and hands that knew nothing but hard work. She wrapped a rough one over his. "You've been more yourself these past weeks than I've seen since before the fire. There's peace to you. You don't say much, but I see it. Never were very chatty. I think you needed to work through that job to put something right in your mind before you could step away."

He levelled a gentle expression at her.

"And have you?"

"As much as anyone can."

"And sometimes that has to be enough."

∞ ∞ ∞

Josh drove out to the big town, leaving Bob with Edie and hoped Barbara didn't kill him. Matt and Willow were already at the hotel waiting for him. Matt had a contract meeting, and Josh hadn't seen Willow for months.

She beamed, easing to her feet, leaning on her cane and hugged him. She was soft and gentle with brown hair and big eyes.

Matt shook his hand. They ordered lunch, and Josh was less self-conscious than he'd been in a while.

"You seem different." Matt appraised him.

He sipped his water.

"Well, well."

"What?" Willow looked from one to the other.

"I met someone." Josh leant in.

"That's so great, who?" She glittered with excitement.

"She's one of our clients." Matt smirked.

"I don't work for you anymore."

Willow tilted her head. "I'm sorry, I wanted to say this for ages. I feel so terrible about what happened to you because of me."

A sad fluttering went through him. He'd had a kicking by a toxic guy in Willow's life. It was the catalyst for change. He knew then he couldn't go on, but he didn't blame her in any way. He was glad she had Matt now. "No, that had nothing to do with you. It was on that arsehole. Really, I'm okay but thank you."

"Good. What's she like?"

He struggled to find the words. "Beautiful. Perfect. Strong but fragile." He tried not to smile.

Matt shook his head. "I'm happy for you."

Josh shrugged it off.

They chatted for a while, and when Willow was tired, Matt took her up to their hotel room and came back, sliding a bag over.

"Belated birthday present from Sel; she asked me to give it to you. And you should go see her. Bea, I mean."

Josh peeled off the tape and sighed. It was a box of condoms with a bow on it. The card in it read *Heard you met someone, so stay safe. You never know, they might come in handy. Love Sel xx*

"What?"

Josh showed it to Matt, who raised his brows.

"Does Sel know you're demi?"

Josh taped the bag shut and gave Matt a wry grin. "No."

"You want me to have a word? Because..."

Josh shook his head, still smiling. "At this point, our friendship consists of her trying to think of people for me to go out with and then me telling her to fuck off. I bet she's loving this."

Matt laughed into his glass with a shake of his head. "Like two kids when you're together."

"Never had a friend like her. I don't mind it because if I told her to back off, she would." Josh should've thrown them away, but for some reason, he shoved the bag in his coat pocket. "How did she know?"

"Mira knows all; Sel doesn't know it's Bea."

"Well, maybe it's for the best." Josh nursed his drink.

"I'm serious. You're free to be with her. She needs friends."

Josh's turned the glass. "I don't know. Sid and Edie need me, and it's more than that. Chadford holds bad stuff for me that goes back years. Since being home for more than a week at a time, I see it. Can't go back, can't take those things on. I'm waiting for my first therapy appointment. I wanted to ask you about what's going on."

Matt sighed. "I can't tell you, you know that. I trust you, and we're friends. It's not my shit to tell. All I can say is she's in a lot of danger, potentially. The investigation is massive, and my only involvement is personal security for her. She plays a small role in a very large picture if what I hear is true. If you were to, say, do a search for Mickey Bennet, I think you might have a better idea of what's what."

Josh swallowed, sweat breaking out. He knew that name. He'd been on the news. He covered his mouth.

"Yeah." Matt turned his glass and sighed before leaning forward. "She's a side player in this, and the truth is, she probably won't end up being involved, but for whatever reason, someone decided she needed to be out of the way."

Rage boiled in his stomach, the acid roiling. Josh shuddered a breath out, trying to centre himself.

"Perhaps it's best you don't have involvement; you look you want to kill someone." Matt almost smirked.

Josh studied his friend with a hard venom in his eyes. "I do."

He needed to leave, think, and calm himself. He pushed his half-drunk beer away.

They said goodbye, and that ugly discord in him lingered, fear for her bit at the back of his mind. Driving helped. Dark country lanes wound, high beams picking up the hedgerows and sharp turns. Josh reached Deerbank just before eleven and picked up Bob, who was still snoring where he left him. Edie was in her robe and nightie, and Sid was already asleep. He said goodnight, and somewhere between at peace and unsettled, he went home. The cottage was cold, and Bob curled up next to him when he got under the covers. The fear he held close for Bea threatened to consume him.

He typed out *Thinking of you. I want to see your face x* and closed his eyes, drifting off to dreams of holding Bea close.

Waking with the hardest boner he ever had, he wasn't used to the desire and need for anyone that seemed to lurk under his skin.

She'd sent him a bed selfie that teased him. The duvet didn't properly cover her body, her hair wild, and he wanted to nudge it down and touch her hair.

You're not helping my morning.

Oh?

He took his own bed selfie, Bob taking up most of the screen. She sent back heart eyes.

His heart hurt. As he waited for the hard-on to go, he stretched his back, needing a piss. He went around in circles, trying to figure out what to do. Go to her or not go to her?

Give into the gnawing urge that would ruin his life?

Drinking coffee, overlooking the valley, he realised he hadn't meditated and gone to the safe place in his mind since he'd been back. He hadn't needed to.

Peace was slowly creeping in him, and he had no idea what to do with it other than war with himself over it.

Run Baby Run

Every night was spent sexting with Josh or on the phone while they told secrets and bared themselves. It was intense and private. Bea had never shared anything like it. Fragile and vulnerable, she opened up to him in ways she never had to anyone. It might've been the distance. It made it precarious and precious. A delicate thread that held strong with words alone.

Each conversation was a deeper, more intimate exploration of desire and themselves, yet there was so much unsaid about their realities. None of it mattered to Bea.

December deepened, and it got colder and grimmer. Christmas came and went, and she had a quiet one with her mum, and she and Josh fell into a routine. Wrapped up in her duvet one night, wearing her cute reindeer pyjamas, Bea and Josh got into a discussion of anal.

"I'm not that fussed on the idea, not that I'm against receiving it."

She almost heard him blink. "Does that mean you've considered giving it?"

"I have given it in the past," she stuttered.

He made a noise in his throat. "That's a thing?"

"Pegging. Before this, I used to prefer being in control." Her heart pounded at the conversation. This was the truth of who she was.

"Control... like, whips and leather?"

She chuckled, the sound of her laugh louder than it used to be. "I never had the urge to live and breathe it or be like a pro-domme, just... I was never passive in sex. Pain never interested me, but leading does. Control but not cruel."

"Tell me what you'd want." His voice went lower.

Her skin goosed. It was a repressed memory of things long given up. The idea of having control or power fuelled her fantasies, but it was a reality that was no longer accessible to her.

Bea sipped her drink. "To be inside you, give you intense pleasure. You to want it, and trust that I'd give it to you. You to obey me and let me guide and lead you. Tease you sweetly. Praise you, and you praise and worship me. Lovingly."

He was breathing hard. "That sounds," he swallowed, "Fucking hot."

She laughed, embarrassed yet elated. "Really?"

"Considering how hard my dick is, yes. It's weird, you bring the sex out in me. I've never felt it, so much desire, but it's that I want to explore it only with you under your guidance and your desire making it mine."

Bea wanted to nuzzle and hold him, but she closed her eyes, pressing against the phone, gripping it harder.

"It's late, lover. You should go to sleep."

"Okay, night." Bea tried to hold onto each precious word from him, but her worry interceded as ever. The relief he gave her kept her afloat, but the reality was she was pent up in constant anxiety.

In the dark, she focused on Josh. The fantasy she played out over and over, lulling her to sleep, but morphed into darker things.

There was no sign of anyone following her, and the investigation was on-going. Yet there was the constant needling in her mind. Always someone after her, and the breath on her neck. What if he got away with it? What if he sent someone after her again? She shut it out and shifted over, focusing on Josh. Bea snuggled into the pillow with warmth in her belly at the mere thought of him and made her smile every time. She wanted to meet him, was desperate to but terrified of asking. She had to stop the merry-go-round in her mind.

∞ ∞ ∞

The morning was grey but dry. Yawning, she dressed for her morning walk. She'd taken to going by herself for ten minutes with one crutch twice a day as it was easier to manage, and her voice was stronger. It was bitterly cold, and her legs ached. She let herself back in, checking behind her, and saw nothing. She was being paranoid; that breath on her neck again.

Her mum was packing when she got back.

"Where are you going?"

"I had an offer on the house before I arrived. Only two thousand under the asking, so I accepted. I didn't say anything in case it didn't work out. They're a cash buyer, and it's all of a sudden going ahead." Paula waved her hands. "I'm going in the morning, sign a few things and organise the house. I'll be a week or thereabouts. I've rung Denbridge, and they're sorting everything out. At least this is sooner rather than later."

Bea stood mutely as her mum's frenetic energy play out. "Right."

Paula sighed. "Sorry. I can go the day after."

"No, might as well get it out the way."

"I'm going to put everything in storage at the place by the motorway, you know the one, and they do removals. I've booked them for the end of the week."

"That's not a lot of time. I can come with you."

"Oh no, dear, no need."

"I'm getting better."

Paula stopped and took Bea by the shoulders. “I know, and you’re doing so well. I’m so proud of you. But honestly, sometimes I’m better focused on my own. It’s not always a good thing. You’re exactly the same.”

Be smiled. They were alike.

“Plus, it’s safer this way. I’ll put your things to be sorted out at a later date. It’s fine.”

Bea hugged her mum goodbye, watched her from the window get in her car and drive off. They were on the third floor with a view of the residents’ car park. It was strange being alone again. She hated it.

At least things were moving. Everything else was a waiting game.

Sel came over that night with a great big pizza and ice cream.

“You don’t have to,” Bea said as Sel whirred past her.

“Bollocks. You’re on your tod, so pizza, film, ice cream.”

“Isn’t this a breach of something?”

“No. I could go sit in my car if you want, but I’m on watch. Plus, I kinda like you.” She shrugged and put the ice cream in the freezer.

The pizza was still hot, and they settled down, picking something to watch. Bea kept checking her phone.

“What’s up with you? You’re glued to that thing.”

Bea tried to play it cool. She didn’t succeed by the expression on Selina’s face.

“Oh, do tell.” She grinned and picked an eighties action film.

“Nothing.”

Selina shifted and stared at Bea, eating her pizza.

“His name is Josh. He was at CAPTA.”

“Wait. Wait. Josh. Our Josh? Growly, long hair, hot as holy fuckery on a Sunday Josh Cotterill is the one you've been talking to all these weeks?” She gave Bea a wicked smile. “That fucker. I knew he was seeing someone.”

Bea went hot and cold. “Um. Yes.”

Sel dropped her pizza slice, wiped her fingers and paused the film. "Everything, I need to hear everything. Because in the whole time I've known Josh, he's never been squirrely with me, I knew it." She shook her head. "And I said to Matt ages ago, has Captain Cagey met someone, and before Matt could deny it, Mira said he was, I was like, nah, the bastard. Wouldn't tell me a fucking thing when I asked. How?"

"He mods the CAPTA support group. We got chatting. You know him well?"

"We worked together a lot. Well, obvs, not now. He's so quiet, I mean, he talked to me, I didn't give him any choice. Neither of us are local, so we'd share a company flat like this when in town. He's kind and sweet, and if he cares about you, he's yours." She picked her pizza up again. "Like a really great puppy."

Bea smiled. Of course they knew each other, but it'd not occurred to her before. "He's helped me."

"I bet he has. I'm happy for you. And him. What's the plan?"

"I don't know. Part of me wants to push to meet him. My life has been on hold for so long, and I'm lucky to be alive. I want to make the most of it."

Sel scowled. "You should ask him to come and see you, but don't be surprised if he says no. And if he does, it's not you."

"Why?"

"He has bad memories of Chadford, and I don't know how much you know, but it's not good for him. The job fucked him up, and I'm glad he left."

Bea chewed the inside of her lip. He'd been pretty vague on the details, and she respected that boundary. "I don't think I like it here either. I mean, it's okay, but I didn't choose it."

"You can go and see him."

"I could. What if I ask and he says no?"

"You have to respect that."

They were quiet, and Bea thought it over, eating until her phone buzzed.

"Is that him?"

"Maybe."

Selina laughed and tried to peek, but Bea hid her phone.

Sel didn't need to, but she stayed on the fold-out and, honestly, it was comforting. Bea spoke to Josh as she got ready for bed, and Sel settled in.

"Hey."

"You know Selina?"

He laughed after a silence. "I do. She knows about us now?"

"I told her. She's watching me while mum is back home."

"You're alone?"

"House being sold. I'm okay."

"Are you?"

Bea swallowed and closed her eyes. "I think so, every now and again, I think someone is there. Just paranoia."

"Tell Sel."

"I was wondering... what if you came down. To visit."

He didn't answer.

"Never mind. Forget I asked. I should go. Night."

He started to say her name, but she ended the call and slumped back in bed. She was a dick.

∞ ∞ ∞

Bea opened the box that arrived two days later. She'd not answered his calls or replied to his messages. She was so embarrassed, she couldn't. He told her it was okay, but he'd not said yes.

For a second, she wondered if he'd come, but a delivery guy handed her a box instead. Inside were some clothes from her mum. Her favourite leather bomber jacket. She shrugged it on and studied herself in the mirror.

She seemed different. Her hair was cared for. Before, she straightened it as often as she left it curly and had straightened it that morning. Her eyepatch was purposeful rather than necessary. She was Bea in a way that she hadn't been for a long time. More confident. She smiled. Becoming more comfortable with herself, her new physicality was familiar and normal to her. The limits were there, but not a hindrance. Part of her.

Yet Bea was different. Some of that was her and the care she received, but some of it was Josh. He gave her an indefinable power, hope? Possibly. Maybe not anymore.

Ignoring that pang of pain, Bea grabbed her bag, slipped on her boots, and went for a walk with a crutch. She texted her mum in the lift, thanking her.

Getting to know her new home, even if she didn't like it much, was important. She had no idea how long she'd be there. She mapped the place in her head, and it was a good way of testing herself. Go left to the Asian supermarket. Right to the Sikh Temple, and that was where the park she liked was. On the main road was the bus stop. The big chain pub that did decent food.

She was so occupied, she didn't see it at first. A car. Black SUV. She'd been followed by one of those before. She focused on her breathing and slowed. The car parked nearby, and Bea turned off the street automatically. It followed. Bea saw the vague outline of the driver. She shuddered, cold and hot at the same time.

Selina had gone through a few routes with her, giving her safe places she could go, and there was a small out of the way pub, The Duke, where she made her way as fast as she could down a one-way road. The SUV would have to go around the ring road to get onto it. At least the ridiculous city road system came in handy for something.

The pub door was heavy and creaked loudly as she pushed her weight into it. Her steps were loud as she cautiously went in. A tall, bald man was behind the bar, who nodded at her as she approached.

"I need, um..." she swallowed.

"Bea, right?"

Bea nodded.

"You can hide here while I call in."

Something made her tense. "No. No need. Just being paranoid... I'll call Selina." She was imagining it, she had to be.

"Well, the back door is unlocked, takes you back through the side streets." He set his hands on the bar.

"Thank you."

With a concerned nod, he moved away.

There were only a few people in the dark, old-fashioned place. The gambler machine pinged and lit up, and she jumped, heading straight through as fast as she could into the ladies.

She shook, standing over the sink. Same car as before, all those months ago that had followed her. Chased her. Even as she doubted herself, Bea was sure of it. She took out her phone, staring at it.

For weeks she'd been hypercautious, flitting from one shitty cash in hand or dodgy job to another, and it was only in the last few months she'd been lax. There was no other choice. Mickey Bennet knew where she was.

She faced herself in the mirror, and something changed. The version of herself she'd become — careful, measured and quiet — vanished. The cold and focused Bea returned. That version had been born of necessity and survival. It'd kept her alive until it didn't. Those weeks were hazy, a blur of fear and the dark. How had they found her? Denbridge had been careful, and the Chadford police had nothing to do with Bennet.

Her phone buzzed in her pocket. Her home and lock screen was the photo Josh sent her of him in the field. She ran her finger over his obscured face. Unlocking it, she hovered over his message. *Can we talk? I miss you.*

Bea nearly did but hesitated. She didn't know how close they'd gotten and cloned her phone for all she knew. Calling anyone or bringing attention to someone in her life could put them in danger. She wanted to call her mum.

She popped out the sd card with her photos, contacts and important info and hid it in her bag. Turning off the phone, she hesitated for a second before tossing it into the bin.

A coldness came back to her, and she shut out the hot sticky breath and presence behind her and pictured the beach with Josh.

Bea put her hair in a ponytail with the hairband on her wrist, then rooted through her bag and set a blue baseball cap on from it. She winced as she took off her eyepatch and put her sunglasses on. Sel had always advised her to keep a first aid kit and disguise with her, though she wasn't sure what good it'd do. Shouldering her bag, she clutched the personal alarm attached to her keys in her free hand and headed through the back exit of the pub, into the beer garden, and out a cast-iron gate.

In the narrow footpath lined with bins, she turned right. It'd take her home but through the back allies of the back-to-back terraces, a remnant of old Chadford, and to the car park and bins at the back of the flats. It wasn't a long walk but felt like miles. She peeked around the corner at the end, leaning on the crutch, seeing the same car parked over the road from her block.

Well, she definitely wasn't paranoid.

She hesitated, centring herself, before moving as quietly as she could. The entrance had the same security as the front, and she put the code in the wrong first and held her breath, willing her hands not to shake, and tried again. Using the stairs so she wouldn't have to go to the front hall for the lift. Her hips screamed. She gritted her teeth and stretched out the cramped joint when she reached the floor. Sweat clung to her even though her face was numb as she reached the stairwell door, and through the toughened glass, she could see her door through it. It was closed. She waited for the lift to ping or any noise. Nothing.

There was no choice. She clung to the keys in her hand with trembling hands to keep them quiet and listened at the door first. No sound. She slid the key in and smoothly opened it. No-one there. She Grabbed her go-bag, as well as some clothes, toiletries and meds, and left the same way. She saw the SUV was still there when she peered around to check. She leant on the wall and took a breath. She needed to get as far away as possible, so she made her way along, passing the pub, which opened onto a busy main road at the end. A bus was already coming down that, heading into the city centre. The crossing peeped, and she hurried as fast as she could, her limp more pronounced with the pain.

Bea used the city pass Sel had organised for her and sat on the nearest seat when she got on the bus. Her ears rung. Sweat pissed out of her. All she wanted was Josh. To hold her. To help her. Then she knew what she was going to do.

If they found her, they'd be watching Denbridge too. And her mum, probably.

"Are you all right, love?" An old man's voice took her by surprise. A few of the other passengers were watching her.

She hadn't realised she was hyperventilating. Breathing through her nose and out through her mouth, she nodded.

The bus terminated at the main bus station. Bea eased into the crowds and to the central train station. There was a phone stand there, and she bought a cheap pay as you go. At the quiet waiting area near the ticket office, she opened it, inserted the sd card and turned it on. Her list of contacts was small, but Josh's number wasn't there. It must have saved to the phone itself.

Bea nearly signed into her social media to message him but hesitated. She had no idea how'd they found her.

She wanted to scream. After ten minutes of quiet yet panicked debate, she got on the internet and searched for Deerbank.

The village was beautiful, settled near a valley. She searched for him through the satellite imaging map, finding the lane and cottage close to what he'd described. She wasn't a hundred per cent sure, but it was the best guess.

The battery was low, and she turned it off, buying a ticket with cash. One change, but she could manage it.

Bea headed to the platform, waiting in the cold din, and nerve pain laced her. She covered her mouth, trying not to throw up. It was three hours on the train, and she could take her meds then. Buying water from a kiosk, she sipped it, agitated, watching everything. A nice woman helped her get on and found her a seat.

Bea had the feeling this was a bad idea. It probably was.

Flurry and Chase

Bea changed trains, groggy from the meds but did it. The day grew dark the further north she travelled, the weather grew grimmer until the first soft, and light snowfall came. By that second one, it was starting to stick, and when she arrived at the station nearest Deerbank, it was falling heavily. She had no idea how to get to the village. There were no taxis.

“Are you all right?” The person who spoke to her had turquoise hair, a thick coat and a warm smile.

“I need to get to Deerbank.” Bea slurred her words.

“I’m passing that way. I can take you, best hurry, the roads will be impassable soon. “I’m Parker. They.”

Bea swayed, trying to focus.

“I’m nonbinary. Okay?” Parker’s wary smile doubled and refocused.

Bea tasted her cottonmouth. “Yes. Sorry. I’m not feeling too good.”

“Here, let me help.” They took Bea’s bags, and they made it to the car. “I live the other side of Deerbank. With weather like this, I don’t think I’ll be able to get to work tomorrow.”

Bea shivered. “What do you do?” She closed her eyes as Parker pulled out into the slow evening traffic.

“Animal sanctuary. Been down to see my partner. They’re at uni.”

“That’s so nice.”

“What brings you up this way?”

"I'm..." Bea went rigid as the pain came back. She wanted to throw up. "Visiting a friend. It's a surprise. Thank you. It's not often people are kind."

"We all need help sometimes."

Bea was half-asleep by the time they reached Deerbank, and it was fully dark and snowy. She'd reserved a room at the pub while on the train, and Parker pulled up outside.

"Need help?"

"No, you get home safe, out the snow. Thank you again."

"Paying it forward." They waved and beeped before easing away.

Bea went into the quiet pub. Busy carpet, beams and dark wood.

"Booked a room." She missed the speech app on her phone as she forced the words out.

The inn was a two-story brewery conversion attached to the pub. She had a ground floor room and opened the stable style door into it. Making sure it was locked first, she took a hot shower before falling into bed after taking more meds.

It was four when Bea woke. She snuggled under the thick duvet, not quite sure where she was. The room was unfamiliar. She sat up, remembering the previous day. It took a moment, and she scrubbed her face. This was what panic and bad decisions looked like. It would've been completely different if she'd checked in like she was supposed to. She huffed a groan. What had she been thinking? She should've gotten the barman to ring to Denbridge. Rational thought had gone out the window. Impulsive-bad-decisions-Bea. That's who she was. She threw back the duvet. There was no point going back.

But that horror lurked. She shuddered, tested her legs, and got up, putting the kettle on. At the window, she slid the curtains open a fraction. Steady snow fell in the dark, casting eerie light, sticking and deep in places.

"Shit."

The car park to the side faced the main road, and there was a shop already open. Hugging the cup of coffee and chomping the complimentary biscuit, she realised how hungry she was. She pulled her jeans on, eased her feet into her long para boots, pulled on the long-sleeved thermal tee and her bomber jacket, just taking her key and some cash.

She moved precariously through the pristine snow, putting her weight on the crutch. The older woman at the shop was shovelling the stuff out front.

"I'm not open, love." She scrutinised Bea, who was sure she was going faint. "You all right?"

"I'm staying at the pub. Not eaten and I... I should eat with my meds."

"All right. Be quick."

"Thank you so much." She winced at the light and grabbed a basket. She picked biscuits, crisps, dried fruit, juice, and a few pre-packed sandwiches.

The shopkeeper put everything in a bag for her, and Bea handed over a twenty-pound note.

"I don't know the area. How long do you think it'll be before the snow is cleared?" Bea stuttered and slurred as she focused on staying upright.

"Oh." The shopkeeper adjusted her glasses. She wore fingerless gloves and a woolly hat. "When it stops, they'll clear the roads. Locals will dig out as much as possible."

"Right. Thanks again." She took her change and lost herself in thought about what to do next, heading back. She really had no idea. As she reached the broad gate, her hair started to get wet from the heavier snow, blizzarding in eerie grey around her. She slowed, taking numbing breaths before seeing her nightmare, and nearly fell. A black SUV parked up, and a silhouetted man peered through the window and knocked on her door.

The inn and pub backed onto a hill with the valley in the distance. She could just make it out through the silent grey squall. Josh was in that direction.

She dropped the bag, and it flumped into the deep snow. Backing up and holding onto the fence, keeping the man in sight, she waded through the snow to the foot of the hill and clambered over the lower fence where it backed onto the pub. Catching her coat on a hawthorn hedge, it tore, and she slipped it off, using her crutch as a pole to move through the deep drift.

Bea climbed, her body screaming in effort as she did, and shivering hard, she looked back. The snow melted into her top and froze her skin. Flakes wet her lips and hair, and the frigid air numbed her senses. She sniffed, gathering her strength. Hidden by the building, she skirted the steep part of the hill and moved toward the woods.

The snow fell thicker until she could barely see anything. Shaking harder, her breath misted in a cloud. Hearing a noise behind her, there was no thought other than run. She hurried, crossing a stile, and moved as fast as she could through the snow, not feeling the pain in her nerves, pulling her stiffer leg behind her, going numb. Each breath burnt ice in her lungs, muscles on fire with pain, heart thudding, and adrenaline fuelled her.

She glanced back, hair plastered over her face, not seeing the dip before her, and slipping, tumbled down a hill into a deep drainage ditch, sinking into the snow, and blacked out.

Into The Woods

Josh was in a foul mood, partly for not sleeping and partly because of Bea. He frowned. Something was wrong. He knew it. She'd not replied to him at all.

The snow was coming in thick flakes that drifted down as he drove up to the cottage with his old pick-up filled with supplies he bought up from the twenty-four-hour giant supermarket off the bypass to wait out the bad weather. At least it was quiet at that time. With his place being elevated and in the position it was, the weather was always worse. The fields were already white.

The narrow B-road curved through farmland and tall hedges, eventually turning up to the small wood on the hill that enclosed him on one side.

He grimaced as the slippy road grew thicker with drifting snow as the wind picked up and slowed further. It was nearly impossible to get down the lane, and he would be cut off for days. Waiting for a second after cutting the engine, he heard Bob barking from inside the house.

It was past when it should be light, but the heavy grey cloud and blizzard rendered everything in grimy pre-dawn darkness. Something was off. Josh couldn't pinpoint why, but something. Maybe the way Bob barked incessantly. He would woof a little if he saw an animal, but he didn't constantly bark at anything. Plus, there shouldn't be anything out there.

Grabbing his scarf, he covered his face and put a cap on, tucking his loose hair behind his ears before finding a torch from the car and clicked on the light, scanning the ground. The snow was pristine. He crunched through it further forward to the edge of the dip, where the garden slid away downward with the trees to his left.

He held his breath. All he heard was the wind. He hovered the torch on the trees beyond his drive and across the spindly trunks. Nothing. He edged out past them and his garden to the hill down into the valley. The snow came harder, and he could barely see but puffed out a breath in the biting air, pulling down the scarf, and saw disturbed snow.

The shallow valley rose again to the east, but west, past the woods and fields, was the village. He spied what appeared to be a person down in a trench at the field's end, lying there. It might've been a tree branch.

Wading down into the snow to get a better look, he slid down the embankment, snow up to his calves in places. The figure was half-covered and unmoving. Definitely a person. Hurrying, he could barely see but reached them. Without wasting time, he clicked off the torch, putting it in his pocket, and hauled them up, leaning their back to him as the wet body slumped against his front.

A woman. With no coat. She'd be lucky if she'd survive in the cold. There was no way he could get her to a hospital. He'd have to take her to the cottage. Shit. Just what he needed. Some random stranger in his home. If she lived.

Bending low and turning her, he hoisted her over his shoulder with a grunt, and instead of going up the hill, he skirted the field back to the shallower incline of the wood, avoiding carrying her up the bank. The going was slow in the heavier snow, which passed his knees, and he growled each breath as he waded. The off-balanced weight and uneven ground were tricky. He hiked her up a few times, her limbs swinging as he did. Her hip pressed into his face, and he shivered at the icy, wet fabric of her jeans. Though the snow was shallow under the trees, it was still a struggle to carry her up the hill, and he slipped a few times but got to the top, his thighs straining in the effort.

When he made it to his cottage, he was out of breath and sweating where he still could.

Josh scowled. Her wet hair covered her face when he leant her against the internal garage wall to find his keys, and with a dropping edge of horror, he pushed the dripping curls out the way. He froze, furious and confused.

It couldn't be. It couldn't. It was.

She wasn't even shivering. Grunting as he opened the door, Josh picked her back up, carrying her in a way he'd fantasised but never thought he would, and not like this.

Under his anger and shock, fear stabbed. Her chest barely rose and fell in shallow even breaths, and her lips took on a bluish tinge. Her beautiful light natural tan skin was ashen.

Bob barked and jumped as he brought her through the cottage and into the kitchen, setting Bea carefully on the rug, pulled down the chair cushions and settled her on them in front of the log burner. Tearing his gloves off, he lit it, hands nearly numb and trembling, but wary of the flame on instinct, he leant away, and as the fire took, he fed it wood.

Josh tossed down his cap and unwound the scarf. He wiped the sweat and moisture of his breath from his face, bracing for what he needed to do.

The glow of warmth was almost pleasant, his body ached and tingled from the cold, but he recoiled as ever and shut the door.

Leaving her, he fetched blankets and towels, along with his first aid kit. Bob whined and followed him, eager to help. He reassured the animal as he moved.

Josh stared down at her, lying on the floor. She'd been part of his life for weeks, and yet in front of him, she was unreal. Shivering and soaked too, he pulled off his coat and jumper, then his boots and jeans, tossing them aside, unable to look away from her.

He knelt. "Hey. Bea." He cupped her face, but she didn't stir. Bob wuffed and nudged her, sniffing all over. "Off." He pointed, and Bob obeyed. "Good boy."

Unlacing her long para boots, he focused, easing them off, before undoing her jeans and wiggling them down. They were so tight and clung to her icy skin. He'd have laughed at the irony of undressing Bea, only for it to be like this, but she was in real danger.

He pulled her top off, her body was limp in his hold, and eased her back. She wore no underwear. He closed his eyes to her naked body, swearing. He spooned her, pulling a towel over her, carefully patting her skin, and then pulling over the fleecy blankets. He wrapped them up, nestling close, shivering from her cold body.

He patted her hair dry while his body ached from the effort, adrenaline ebbing, and his body warmed as she did. Josh closed his eyes with her cradled in his arms. Bob settled in front of her, curling up with his head on her thigh, and whined, setting his doleful eyes on Josh.

"Good boy," he whispered.

His feelings, unexpected and filled with fear, encroached with the need to never let her go. He couldn't lock the emotion down and let out a silent sob as he held her tighter, and in the glow of the firelight, he uttered silent prayers for her to be okay; he promised anything asked of him. He could not lose her. He couldn't. The prayer became a chant until lulled and exhausted, he drifted off.

He knew she was awake. Awareness shifted in him. The day was dull, snow falling hard. He eased his arm from under her head and tucked her in. Bob was fast asleep, letting out a gentle snore. The fire was nearly out, and Josh squatted, putting new logs in.

"I know you're awake."

He heard the rustle of movement.

"Josh."

He closed his eyes, fighting the tears that would choke him. He left the room. Dressing in fresh clothes, he selected some sweats, a vest and thermal socks and took them to her.

She was stroking Bob, all wrapped up the covers, her hair wild. She was more than beautiful. He couldn't draw breath at the idea of going to her, taking her in his arms, and finally kissing her. Sparkling dark eyes full of life, soft skin, a figure that he wanted to cling to... not that he was looking.

"Are they for me?" she whispered in a dry rasp.

She gazed straight at him, lips parted, pale, clutching at the blankets. She hadn't flinched. Of course she wouldn't.

"I'm so cold."

Gathering himself, he set the clothes down.

"Help me. I'm stiff, and I hurt." Bea stuttered her words.

Her voice nearly undid him. His hands shook as he slipped the vest on her, carefully easing it over her head and arms, fingers brushing her skin. All the while, she watched him. He let her.

A long-sleeved top, then a sweatshirt, and it swamped her. She leant forward, tucking her hands into the sleeves. "Thank you."

"Don't thank me. How did you get here? How did you find me? Why?"

The light in her eyes vanished, and she swallowed hard, glancing outside. "How isolated are we?"

"Very," he rasped. "Snow like this will mean we're trapped."

She chewed her lip. "Someone's after me."

With a Wolf

Bea was torn. Relieved and elated. Devastated she'd let him down. When she'd woken, she was so deliciously warm. Awareness interrupted her peace as her body throbbed and ached. Evil dreams lingered, letting fear hover at the edge of consciousness.

No, something else. Oh, the person holding her. She held her breath, staying calm, and blinked into wakefulness. Her body pulsed with pain as she took a breath.

She faced a smouldering fire of white ash over glowing embers. A fan whirled on the stove, and the room was perfectly warm. Pinned by a huge arm, she let herself fix the feel of his body. Rough skin pressed against her, and her head rested on the firm expanse of the other arm, hard muscle cradling her. And Bob was nestled and snoring in front of her.

Holding back a sob, she bit the inside of her cheek. Josh had found her. Her face contorted with emotion, but she pulled it back and resisted the urge to snuggle into him as it almost overcame her. She let out a steady breath, blinking tears back, and swallowed it all down. His chest rose and fell behind her, soothing her.

In the dim room, she made out the neat stack of logs, discarded clothes, but she couldn't move. She didn't want to. She wanted to enjoy the precious moment before it was gone. She luxuriated in the sensation of his skin on her face, the weight and form of him, the body pressed against her back, and the scent of faded deodorant and his own smell, not strong but musky and so good. She took a deep breath and smiled.

Josh shifted. Bea closed her eyes, not ready for things to change and fearing the inevitable. The man behind her sighed and carefully lifted her head, extracting his arm. He felt her hair with a grunt that went through her body.

When he'd moved away, she nearly cried out at the loss. He tucked the layers of blankets back over her, and she cracked open an eye when his presence was gone. Naked other than for his boxer briefs, he squatted in front of the fire and put on another log and opened and closed the grate, making it scrape. The flame took. Shadowed, broad shoulders and long hair filled her vision.

Thick scars over pale skin covered the one side of his back, disappearing under the waistband of his moulded underwear and wrapped over his shoulder and down his arm. She knew they followed on his chest and face. He was everything and more. When he left the room, she knew the wrongness of what she'd done.

"Explain it." He un-balled socks.

He was closed down. Distant. She told him everything, easing on the sweats under the covers, and he put the socks on, tucking the bottoms into them for her. It was like she was wearing a duvet.

"In the village?" The amber hue of his eyes made her think of a wolf. The gaze of a predator, and she wanted to be devoured by him. He vibrated with fury.

Her voice failed her, and she only nodded. She wasn't sure how they could've followed. Her bank? Had she been followed to the station, or they already knew about Josh? Did it matter?

He got up, moving around the kitchen. Bob whined and thumped his tail, and she focused on the animal. Bea put her hand to her mouth, turning to the window, and the storm raging silently outside other for than the low whistle of the wind. Josh was everything she hoped. The discoloured skin grafts and uneven scars on the one side of his face, marred top lip — making him seem like he was sneering — and half his eyebrow and ear missing didn't diminish him, but they were a fixed detail of his life. He was gorgeous. Hers.

She was stiff and sore and really wanted to sleep. Glancing at him, she amended that thought. Mostly sleeping. Some snuggling. Maybe kissing. But not after what she'd done to him.

He left and returned with shopping bags, setting the groceries out, laid the table, and started cooking.

He gave her a big mug of strong, hot tea that was probably half sugar in silence. The wooziness eased as she sipped it and cradled the hot cup.

"What are you thinking?" Bea managed in a whisper, desperate to know.

"I'm attempting to process the fact you are in my home. Like, actually sat there." He closed the cupboards and tidied up before setting bowls of soup down.

Bea tried to stand but couldn't.

Josh stopped and helped her, and she found his arms around her, holding close. The room spun, and her head hurt, and side hurt. She felt like she'd been a rugby ball for a day.

With a swallow, he virtually carried her to the table. The silence grew uncomfortable as he joined her, and she scoffed the food.

"We should talk about what happens now."

Bea watched him for a minute and put her spoon down.

"They won't be able to drive here until the snow is cleared." He sipped tea, lost in thought. "That means they'll be on foot. It'll be impossible to climb in the snow now without knowing where they're going, so I guess they'll wait it out. They'll have to go through the woods when they figure out where you are. The moment the snow stops, we need to act."

"How long?"

"Depends on how deep the snow is." He pressed his lips together, examining everything but her.

The shame of her actions rose like bile, and she suddenly felt sick. "Would you mind if I went to bed?"

He widened his eyes and opened and closed his mouth a few times.

She gazed at him in question.

Panic crossed his face, but with a clenched jaw, he put his arm around her and led her to the stairs. Bea's breath misted in the frigid cold.

She let him help her upstairs, struggling with stiff joints and her weak leg. The narrow stairwell turned against the wall leading to landing and large arched picture window, looking out onto the countryside.

Bea paused. Snow flurried and whirled, the wind catching it up in the gloaming. It was barely afternoon. The view was of nothing but chaotic white in front of thick grey dark.

"We're trapped here."

"We are." The rasp in his voice close to her ear made her want to clear her throat. "We'll be safe."

"But I can't leave." She shivered and sweat prickled, and she couldn't tear her gaze away from the storm.

A board creaked, and she craned her head up, seeing him shrouded in shadow. The wind screeched from somewhere. He appeared hurt.

"I get claustrophobic."

He fought a smile. "I'm sorry." Josh held her tighter. "I won't touch you, I won't do anything, but there's only one bed."

Her shivering worsened, and she clung to his warmth. In a room off the main landing, he flipped on the light. Bob trotted in behind them and jumped on the bed.

The room was finished in tasteful and beautiful neutral tones with wooden furniture. He closed the heavy curtains and opened a latched door.

"Bathroom."

She peeked and nipped in and washed up. At the sink, she realised there was no mirror.

"I'll leave you to it," he said when she went back into the bedroom. He clutched blankets and a pillow in front of him.

Bea's disappointment must have shown.

"You'll be safe. No one is coming here yet."

"I don't want to be alone."

"It's not a good idea." He clicked on an electric heater.

"Why?" Her teeth chattered harder. "It's too cold to be alone. Keep me warm." Her voice failed, and she eased into bed, heart thudding.

Josh's jaw worked hard, and he put the pillow and blanket down. "Bea, this... coming here..." he sat on the bed. "This wasn't okay. I'm not prepared. Finding you like that." He picked at the duvet.

"I'm so sorry, and I accept that, but I'm still so cold."

He turned away, and his shoulders rose and fell before he slid in next to her, lying still and rigid, perching on the edge.

Bea dithered harder. Josh shifted Bob as he nudged him from the middle spot of the bed. Her eyes adjusted to the dark, and he stared at the ceiling.

"Josh, hold me."

She made out the pain in his face before he turned to her. His scars buried in the pillow, hair everywhere.

She smiled at him. "This isn't how I saw the first time we share a bed."

"No."

Shifting closer, she could almost kiss him but didn't, and made her voice work. "I hope you can forgive me one day. But I understand if you can't." She turned, and they snuggled. He was the perfect big spoon. Silence lay thickly as they warmed, the sensation of his body against hers was heaven, and she wanted to cry.

Big arms encased her, and she breathed in time with his light rasp, relishing his warmth and the smell of him on the sheets and clothes.

She had missed something she'd never experienced all her life, and her heart ached now she had it, but it wasn't hers, not anymore. With a sigh and regret, she closed her eyes, knowing she'd ruined everything to stay safe.

Lights Out

Josh smelt her hair. He fought the urge to breathe it in forever, kiss the skin on her neck and shoulder. He wanted her. His skin prickled at the sensation and let the feeling smooth over him until it peaked and abated. There was just new desire lurking within him with Bea in his arms. In his actual arms.

He couldn't help it. He nuzzled her. Her breathing deepened and regulated, and he smiled. She relaxed in his hold and trusted him enough to sleep.

She was safe and with him. The desire to keep her that way was his priority, but he knew the truth.

Anger followed. Anger at her circumstances. Fury at the people who'd hurt her. That he was the means to an end for her. She might like him, but he understood. He could help her. Protect her. If her pursuer was in the village, he could make them disappear. He knew how to make sure they'd never be found. He tensed, pushing away the ugly thought and breathed deep. She could use him and project onto him. He got it. It hadn't been the first time he'd drawn that kind of attention, and he'd never responded, but she'd been different. He thought, at least.

It was wonderful to have her in his arms. The strength and humour he'd come to admire and the vulnerable sweetness of her. Of all the fantasies he had of being able to meet her, this wasn't one, not by a long way. He couldn't stop feeling it as he held her, and he willed himself not to shake.

"Bea." His rasp was barely aloud, but she exhaled, and he swept her hair over to the side, unable to not touch her. The sweetness of her moan was nearly too much.

It was exquisite.

She settled, and he wound a curl through his fingers — he remembered that conversation and how much he itched to do it, and here he was, playing with it, and then he planned everything through, countering every possibility. Things had irrevocably changed between them. The delicate balance shattered, but that could wait. His anger didn't matter. Keeping her safe did.

"Are you asleep?" Her quiet voice made his heart skip.

"Yes."

She shuffled over and snuggled into the pillow. The duvet covered all of her except her nose and curls.

Josh slid his hand out and smoothed her hair back. If she were a cat, she'd purr. He smiled.

"You're the first person that I talk to when I feel down. I feel down."

Josh kissed her forehead, unable to not give her that sweet comfort. He ached at doing it. "Sometimes, things happen and get in the way. I wish things were different for us."

Her face lost all expression. Something bittersweet in her gaze. And when she spoke, there was no resentment or anger, just sadness and regret. "I shouldn't have come. You never wanted me here and said no before." Her words faded to a whisper, and the guilt in her eyes before she closed them hurt him.

He didn't have the words to explain it. "I never actually said no. We never talked about it."

She opened her eyes and watched expectantly.

"My answer was, I don't know. Not because I didn't want to meet. I wasn't sure if I could. Maybe eventually, but you took that choice away. I get it... circumstances, we'll never know."

Her face contorted, and she stuttered a hoarse whisper when she spoke. "I'm sorry. I always make the wrong choices. I planned to call but my phone..." She couldn't get the words out and scraped her bottom lip into her mouth. With a breath, she spoke on the exhale. "If you'd have said no, I'd have left you alone, I swear."

"How do you feel about seeing me now, scars and all?"

Blinking, she gathered her emotion in. "I love them because they're part of you and who you are. You've given me so much." Bea slid her hand to his face, smoothing her fingers through his hair with nothing but warmth in her eyes. They were more expressive than he could've hoped. She inched closer to his mouth as he pulled her flush against his body.

"I violated our trust." Her eyes shimmered with tears. There was no volume left in her voice, and she tried to pull away.

He didn't answer, not letting her go, holding tighter, and his breath whispered on her skin in the silence.

"We're trapped here for who knows how long. Is this all we have? What about after?" She sounded so quiet and fragile as her lips nearly brushed his.

As much as his heart hurt, he didn't have the answers. "I don't know."

"That's fair." The moment passed, she smiled softly and turned back over.

For the first time, he'd been ready to trust, and he had no idea what he felt anymore. He'd be angry if she wasn't so hurt. "I'm sorry."

"Me too."

Josh didn't move, almost numb, watching her nap on and off until she woke properly as the day faded.

"Can I shower? Feel wretched," she mumbled after finally waking properly.

In silence, he got her to the bathroom. She was in so much pain, she could barely walk. He helped her undress as the water warmed. A few bruises dotted her, and he wanted to soothe the aches and take them from her. Her wide eyes were set on him, fluttering, shivering, and naked. He couldn't move as he tried not to look at her bared form.

She pushed her hair back from her face, and he caught sight of her scar. He reached out, his hand hovering. Anger and pain at what she'd gone through properly registering in him.

"It's okay." She shivered.

He stepped back and left her to wash.

Josh listened to her sobbing as he waited on the landing, unsure what to do with himself until the sound hurt too much. The water turned off, and he dithered a few minutes and knocked on the bathroom door.

She was struggling to clean her teeth and got toothpaste everywhere. He helped her — not taking her in as much as possible, closing all that down in his mind — to clean up and get dry and dressed. She smelt like his soap and wore his clothes, and it appealed to something base and primal in him. With his heart turning in the stilted silence, he clicked up the heater and left her to rest with Bob keeping guard of her.

Downstairs, he checked his phone, seeing texts from Sid. He texted back he was safe and had supplies and called Matt.

"How's the storm? Everyone's losing their shit over it." He sounded tense and distracted.

"Bad. In a snow globe."

Matt laughed briefly but sounded like he was moving about.

"Bea's here."

"Thank fuck. She okay?"

"She was followed. Fled here. Found her in the snow half-dead. They're in the village. Are you still working her security?"

Matt sighed in exasperation. "We are. Supposedly, but she vanished. Selina thought she'd gone to her mum in Brakton, but she never got there, and she's been trying to trace her. I think she's currently bollocking Tommy at The Duke. I was about to call you to ask if you knew. I guess Bea didn't know who to trust."

"Yeah." His belly churned. All those people to help her and she chose him.

"Was she hurt?"

"Scared. Hypothermia."

"Who followed her?"

"She thinks it's the man who drove her off the road before."

"I'll deal with it. You keep her safe. Her coming to you is significant. You'll just have to entertain yourselves while you're stuck there."

Josh grunted and ended the call.

He was the only person Bea truly trusted and wanted in this crisis. Of course she'd come to him to keep the others safe. More than that, she needed help and wanted him to do it, he was the one to help her, and he'd bloody well do it. No matter what.

It was enough.

Bad Girl

The realisation of the mistakes she'd made piled into her thoughts the moment she stood under the water. Desperate to clean her teeth, she'd turned off the shower and found toothpaste and a spare toothbrush, and as she scrubbed, nosed through the vanity for hair product. He couldn't have perfect hair without using anything on it. She only found leave-in conditioner, which she used, and a massive box of condoms hidden in a small bag nestled among various emollients and salves. Maybe she'd been wrong about him. She scowled, licking toothpaste residue from her teeth, and put them back where she found them as he knocked on the door.

Bea kept thinking about those condoms in between bouts of crying as she fell asleep. Her eyes were swollen and sinuses blocked when she woke from her nap. She stared at the clock next to her, massaging the bridge of her nose. The minute changed, and stretching her neck, she got up. Even with the electric heater, it was freezing. She leant against the sill at the small window, massaging her hip and watching the fields of white beyond and the snow falling silently and trying to ignore the stabbing pain in her eye.

How could she have done this to him? She should've gone to Sel. It would've been fine. She massaged her temple with the heel of her hand and grunted, shaking it off. She was there now, and it was done. Couldn't be undone, and she would just have to live the consequences of losing him. She deserved no better for what she'd done.

With a deep sigh, Bea pulled off the towel on her head, finding her hair dry and marginally less nest-like, and absently tidied and wound the curls with her fingers, staring at the bitter landscape as what light there was faded.

Shivering, she turned from the view and gingerly made her way downstairs when she realised it was nearly dark.

Josh was cooking, and her mouth watered.

"Hi." He turned from the range, and it was hard for her to look at him; it made her heart pinch.

She offered him a flat smile and walked past him as he tracked her. Every time she saw him, guilt punched her in her chest. The snowfall lightened and drifted nearly to her waist as she stood at the window. The sky was black and everything dark, and a sea of white left the landscape devoid of colour. It was bland and cold, and she didn't like it.

"We'll be here for a few days. Forecast says more's coming. You can rest."

"I don't need to rest. I should leave." She turned, and he looked like she'd punched him.

"You've been crying." He barely said it aloud.

Bea turned back to the night outside. "I'm all right now, thank you." They were out there, so close to getting to her, and the only thing between was the storm. She trembled. It was unbearable.

"Are you sure you're okay?"

"Yes." It sounded unconvincing to her ears, but she didn't care anymore. The fear and desperation overwhelmed her. Tired didn't cover it. Bone-weary.

Her breath caught, and she sat on the floor in a heap. Now the hope she'd held onto, Josh, was gone, and her illusions shattered. She'd hurt him and herself. It was over for her, and there was no way to win.

Bea covered her mouth to stem the high-pitched sob that gathered in her throat. She tried to hold back the panic, but it bubbled over all at once.

Josh knelt next to her, but she only shook her head.

"It's cold here, come sit by the fire."

She nodded but couldn't move and trembled.

He grabbed a blanket and covered her with it, staying by her side, not touching her. They watched the snow fall heavier, and she swayed.

"Lean on me."

She did. He pulled her close and held on with his arms tensed around her, and she sucked the strength from him. He ran a soothing hand down her back and, shuddering a breath, set her on his lap, cradling her with her head on his chest. His body and warmth made her feel small and safe, and she clung to his scent and heartbeat.

Bea fought off the bitterness that told her he didn't want her. He wasn't hers. The longer she stayed in his hold, the harder it was to pull away. It was a wrench, but she made herself lean back.

"I need a drink."

"Drink or drink, drink?"

"Drink, drink."

"Hmm. Let's see."

Bea crawled over to the fire, and he came back with two glasses of dark liquid.

"Rum."

She took a sip. "This is terrible." It burnt as it slid down her throat.

"All I got." He gave a weak smile.

He finished making dinner, the smell of food appealed to her primal need, and she came around from her daze.

She ate the pasta, heavy with cheese like a woman possessed when he handed the bowl to her.

Josh hadn't started his but held the dish, staring at her.

"What?" she asked around a gobful. It was delicious with mushrooms and spinach and cheese.

One side of his face curled up into a smile, and he made a sound that could have been a laugh and shook his head, tucking into his own.

"You're a really good cook."

"I think you hit your head."

Bea smiled and sipped her rum. Full, having eaten too quick, she stared at the flames.

He swallowed, clearing his throat. "You caught me on the back foot. I was surprised. It'll be okay."

With a nod, she picked up her bowl again and ate some more. She glanced at him occasionally, wondering if she'd heard him right. But she couldn't hope.

Later, when Josh had cleaned up, he grabbed the cushions and blankets and made them a nest, feeding the fire. Bea couldn't get warm even with Bob nestling up to her. She absently stroked his head as he snored.

She closed her eyes and saw snow.

"Do you want to read?"

Bea took a book from the pile nearby — a romance, which made her smile inwardly — and, curling up on her side, sipped her rum and read. It was peaceful and snuggly and safe.

He took a book, perching reading glasses on, and read himself. In any other situation, it would have been perfect.

When Bea realised she'd read the same page eight times or more, she gave up, tucking herself into a ball. She liked watching the fire and focused on Bob, who took a deep, snoring sigh.

The air was weighted with tension. She wasn't sure how to wait it out for the next few days, but it wasn't going to be much longer, was it?

"This is almost perfect, isn't it? But I wish I'd never come."

Weariness filled the slow sigh he let go, and his shoulders slumped. "There are days when I forget what my voice sounded like before. Speaking is hard. You're usually the only one I really talk to. Look at me."

She did.

"I'm this. Alone and cut off."

"I was a game, so you could feel like you were before?"

"No." He set his book down.

"You were constant and kind. Everything I needed and thought I was that for you. You made love to me. Was that real for you?"

"Yes," he snapped.

She only stared at him, fixing his image in her heart, unable to speak.

"But see what I'm saying." His voice descended into a growl.

"Are you talking about your scars?" Bea whispered.

"No, I'm..." He clenched and unclenched his jaw. "It's more complicated than that. I know how I look and know that it doesn't make me ugly. But it's more than surface for me, and I can't explain it."

Bea wanted to kiss him, or more precisely, she wanted him to kiss her. The words of need and lust they'd shared and promises made that lay unfulfilled. "I see the man I want and care deeply for." She got up with difficulty, taking her glass into the kitchen, and topped it up.

Josh followed and stood too close, shadowed and sharp in the dimness. "I want you, of course I want you. I want to be everything you've needed. I can't give it to you."

Bea scraped her lip between her teeth as she turned to face him, so weary she held onto the surface behind her to stay standing. It had nothing to do with their relationship but what she'd done. "Sorry, I understand, I didn't mean to push." The urge to fight for them and beg forgiveness made her throat ache.

Josh moved even closer with his stare fixed on her. Colour filled his unscarred cheek as his eyes dipped to her mouth. Bea leant back as his lips parted. In a sudden movement, he broke away and refilled his own glass.

Bea blinked furiously and swallowed. The wind howled outside.

Josh turned the glass and slid it away. His chest rose and fell sharply, and he gripped the worktop. "I've never been in a relationship before."

"Okay," she said slowly.

"I was twenty-six when I was in the fire. I'd never had a partner. I never met anyone I liked that way. Never spent time with enough people to find anyone. Women came onto me, but I couldn't. I tried kissing, and it was so odd. I couldn't understand people around me going after people for sex. I thought back then it was because things had been hard for me. I even tried going to this gay pub. Just nothing. I didn't feel anyone could understand me or my life. It's hard to connect with anyone."

"Wait. Never?"

"No. Never." He cleaned up. "So, you know, I'm not, it's not... you're the first person I've ever wanted to be with. Sexual attraction isn't something I experience much. At all. I told you I was demi." He shuffled for a minute, muttered something and left.

She shrugged her mouth down, nodded to herself and finished her rum.

Sweeping a blanket over her shoulders, she searched him out, using the furniture or walls to support herself. In a small room off the hall, he was on a treadmill, pounding it hard. One side was filled with building supplies with no plaster on the walls.

He ignored her.

Bea put all her energy into her words. "Do you think that bothers me? The things you've said, it felt like we did them."

He kept running.

"Stop, please. Josh."

The light went out, and the treadmill slowed. Neither moved in the dark and quiet.

"Fuck it," he said finally.

"Did I do that?" she stuttered in a whisper.

He laughed. "Solar panels have gone."

Bea clutched the blanket tighter.

"When the snow stops, I can get up and clean it off. It means there'll be no hot water either."

Bea pressed her lips together and held out her hand, searching for him in the gloom, and there was only the light reflecting off the snow. She saw him in the eerie light transfixed as she felt out for him and heard the rasp of his breath and the wind screeching outside.

"If you don't want to have sex with me, that's fine. No one said we had to be physical, and I won't push you for anything. We just have to get through the night, and I can see about leaving tomorrow, maybe. Then it'll be over with."

Josh couldn't hide the pain in his face in the weak, pale light and took her hand when he stepped down off the treadmill. "Is that what you want?"

"No. But it's what needs to happen."

Josh lowered his face, and she couldn't see it. In silence, he helped her back through and went into the utility and found a few oil lamps, wind up torches and a box of candles. He passed her the box, and they went back to the fire. She lit the candles she fixed into the double candelabra on the sideboard as he lit a lamp, and the room glowed with warm light.

She smiled to reassure him, pulling a blanket around her shoulders as she sat by the fire. Bob lifted his head from his beanie bed but went back to sleep.

He kept watching her from where he stood at the sideboard, gripping the edge of it, and his gaze caressed her body, every second heavier with tension. She wasn't sure how they'd get through the next hour, never mind the night.

"Bea." His brow was furrowed, and he pushed off and walked to her.

She didn't speak.

"You are stuck here. And I do feel this. Intensely... and I..." His head fell forward, and she waited as he wrestled with something.

Bea read him. He was angry with her but wanted her. She'd give him whatever he wanted.

Josh sat next to her and made them a nest. He tucked her hair behind her ear and tilted his head. "How do you..."

"What?" she breathed, unwilling to move lest she broke the spell.

"Kiss?"

Her heart burst, and she clenched every muscle so she wouldn't just leap on him. The pull of that desire to take and control itched, but she didn't and aimed an even gaze at him. "We can find out if you want."

Eye of The Storm

Josh reached out, more nervous than he ever imagined possible, and ran his hand down her cheek. He leant in. "I don't know how."

Bea's mouth quirked up, and she urged his head closer until their mouths touched. Soft, warm lips met his, and she moved them lightly, her tongue flicking into his mouth in play. He mirrored her, and she moaned as he slipped his hand around her waist. His nerves vanished.

The hot and wet exploration of her mouth was strange but more than pleasant. The one time he'd tried it, he'd almost recoiled. Her full, soft lips worked with his, so good to finally have her in his arms. He didn't care about the rest of it because this was perfect. The exciting newness of her tongue and lips and sensations of unexplored closeness consumed him.

They parted, and he stared at her mouth.

"Are you okay?"

Her low and quiet voice brought him around. "Yes." He leant in and kissed her again, and they fell into the nest of cushions.

Their bodies pressed together. Feeling bold, he ran a hand from her waist up to beneath her breasts. The soft touch of her warm skin and the beating heart within all were real. They parted, and he placed his hand flat on her chest, relishing the steady thump under his touch and the tremor to her breath.

She was right there, and he could be with her. His breathing kicked up, and the pressure in his dick sent pleasure through his body.

He swore he wouldn't allow this to happen. He needed to back away. Bea hummed, and the sound undid him. The tension became thick, and desire crackled between them.

Josh clenched his jaw.

She speared her hands through his hair. "You are completely free to explore what you want or stop."

His lips parted, and he held her tighter, unable to fight. "Thank you."

She slid her thigh over his hip, and he held it, massaging her muscle as they kissed deeper. Weeks of denied lust and want poured out between them. His lips spoke, his touch told her it had all been real, giving her what he wanted to say. Every word between them was an ideal truth. It was theirs.

Josh rolled her onto her back, and she locked her legs around his hips, and he ground into her. He caressed everywhere and kissed down her neck, his desire breaking free to share something perfect with her.

"I want you." He kissed down to her breast.

"Wait."

Josh froze, panting over her and pleasure skittering through him.

"This is fast. Not for me, I want to jump your bones, but for you."

His lips tingled, and he pulled them into his mouth.

"We can slow down. I'm okay with this not being sexual. I don't want you to feel obliged."

Her voice brought him back to himself. If this was it, the only moment they had, he needed to take it. There would never be anyone else for him. Heartbreak could wait. His lips brushed her cheek as he held onto her. "I want you if you do."

"That's not how this works. I need you to want this as much as me." Her voice faltered and scraped as she forced the words. He knew how hard it was for her to speak.

As she lay beneath him, he relived every moment they shared when he first got to know her. The exciting newness of the things they said to each other. It had been so precious and fragile to him. He'd guarded it close to his heart as she took up space there. He'd not really considered it as a physical thing where the outline of it was harder to touch.

She had. It was tangible and real to them both but in different ways. Yet with her right there, her heart beating, skin warm, and her hard lines that were soft to his touch Josh did want it. If he was to be with anyone, it was her. He knew it'd only ever be her.

Bea caressed his face and pulled away. "We should stop and be sensible."

"No, no." He cleared his throat. "I might have committed to memory what you said once about oral. I'd like to make you come."

She laughed and bit her lip. "Really?"

He grunted, moved away, heart pounding, put another log on the fire and closed the curtains. He pulled her by the hips so they were closer to the stove. It was uncomfortable being near the heat, but he didn't want her to get cold.

Josh pushed up her jumper, frowning at the bruises. "Are you in pain?"

"I'm a bit tender but okay. Looks worse than it is. Promise."

He swallowed, running his fingers down her front. "I'll be gentle."

She licked her lips and tried to speak but shook her head in frustration and tried again. "Show me."

The ache in his dick was unbearable, and he wasn't sure he liked the feeling but focusing on her, he leant down, pressing kisses under her navel until he reached the waistband.

He gripped the bottoms and pulled them off. He stared, transfixed. She was beautiful.

Bea nudged him with her knee.

"Hmm." He settled between her legs, licking his sensitive lips as his mouth watered. Her knees opened wide, letting herself be vulnerable to him. He was going to taste her, see her come, and she was perfection. He didn't breathe, fixing her in his mind. Measuring himself, he braced for everything to change, to give her all he could, watch her pleasure, and tamped down the raw, vulnerable feeling in his heart. He pressed his hips into the bunched fabric under him to halt his want.

Josh slid his hands over her legs, kissing to her thighs, just as she'd described to him. The scene she'd created in his mind was so intense, he came from it. It was the first time another person had made him come. It was so new and yet familiar. He was certain with her because they'd already done this.

He skimmed up her sides, and she panted. He went under the sweatshirt and stopped when he reached the underside of her breasts.

She arched up to his touch. "Please."

He kissed the inside of her thigh still, licking the skin, savouring every moment of it, and when he changed thighs, she squirmed.

"I'm being gentle," he said against her skin. But it was so much more than that. Josh needed to savour the moment, every second of touching her was precious, not just for her pleasure or his memory, but this was a vital moment for him; connecting with someone he cared for and exploring physical pleasure.

"If you don't touch me right now..." she moaned, thighs trembling.

"You'll what?" He spoke over her wet heat with the taste of her already on his lips.

Salivating at her scent, feeling drunk, he swallowed before lightly licking her clit. She lifted her hips into the air and cried out. "Yes, up, there."

He followed her instructions, remembering what she'd told him. Softly yet firm.

Heaven.

Holding tight with his arms over her body as he cupped her breasts, full in his hands, he licked and sucked and kissed her soft, sweet pussy. The light tang of her taste, wetness over his lips, and the sounds she made; moaning and hissing her breath as her body tensed, all became too much. He wanted to come. The pleasure pressed in, and he tried to concentrate on the soft texture between her lips, learning the map of it, working out what she liked the most.

Bea liked a soft, flat downward motion and a circular suck and kiss back up.

She trembled, her breathing ragged, and she tensed. He let her go, licking his lips, needing to see her.

Bea seemed drugged. "Too close, please."

He gave her what she wanted.

Settling back down, this time he held her thighs, delighting in them around his head, and she took over caressing her breasts, and he moaned gruffly, half watching her as she arched, shaking, and then he felt it. The muscles contracted against his lips, spasming, and her body bucked. She ground into his mouth, crying out. He held on, letting her ride it out.

Bea was glorious. She slumped down, and he let her go. She panted, eyes closed.

Fuck, he wanted to do it again. He wanted to watch and feel her come forever. It was so awing to experience so much pleasure. His heart pounded.

Josh glanced up, his head still between her thighs, and crawled up between her legs.

With heavy lids, she pulled him down, and she kissed him deep and hard, taking her taste from him. The impatient need in his groin grew uncomfortable, and he ground against her. He stopped abruptly, knowing if he didn't stop, he'd come.

"What?" she breathed into his neck, kissing his scarred side.

Josh cradled her tight. "I'm... I need to..."

"I can suck your dick? Or use my hand. If you want, you can be inside me."

He stopped breathing, and his skin prickled though he was starting to sweat. The notion of sliding into her consumed him.

He itched to tell her what this meant, how much he cared for her, no, loved her. Because he did. He held her in his arms, and he loved her.

"Josh?"

"I want you."

Neither of them spoke for a few minutes. The wind howled, and fire crackled. Bob snored. He didn't know what to do.

When he leant up, she blushed.

"I was nosy before and found those condoms in your bathroom." A playful but sweet light played in her eyes.

He pressed his face to hers. "Oh god. When Sel figured out I was seeing someone, she gave them to me as a joke. I'm glad I didn't throw them away."

Bea started laughing, a full but quiet laugh as she threw her head back, and it did something pleasant in his dick, and he ground against her again. She hummed and pushed him off. Darting out into the cold, taking a lamp, Josh went up to get them. It was almost a relief. He could back out, he didn't need to do this, and she wouldn't be upset with him. Part of him knew that it would make everything more complicated. Perhaps it was selfish of him, but he needed a connection. Her connection. Maybe they could make it work. Maybe there was hope.

He returned, freezing, and he pulled her into his arms, covering them up and rubbing her back. Warming against her, Bea's mouth was close to his, and she smiled, gaze fixed on his lips.

"Absolutely sure?" she whispered.

"Yes."

She hummed before pulling his bottom lip into her mouth with a soft suck. He kissed her greedily, lust crowding his thoughts, and he needed to touch her.

Bea's movement slowed him, and he followed her guidance. Over and over, their tongues caressed until his lips tingled.

The pressure became unbearable.

She smiled and cradled his scarred cheek.

"You truly want me?" He frowned.

"Right now." She steadied her breath, and reached out to him, grabbed the hem of his sweatshirt and lifted it.

Josh hesitated but nodded. She sat up, running her hands over his chest. He could only watch as she skimmed over his smoother skin and then the scars under his top. No one had ever touched him in desire, with lust, and the only people who'd touched him since the fire were doctors and nurses.

He held her hands still and closed his eyes.

"We can stop."

He smiled. "No, I'm ready." He reared back and pulled off his top, showing her his body.

She gave him a small, wicked smile and pulled off her own. His gaze flickered over her hard, dark nipples and the lovely curve of her waist.

Bea held her hand out, and he went down to her, kissing again, and she caressed his back, wrapping her legs around him, pushing his sweats down with her foot. He raised up on his arms, putting distance between them.

"I want you so much, you feel so good." Her hands caressed him, running over his body.

He moaned.

"You're so fucking sexy. Just," reaching around, she squeezed his bum, "so hot, every inch of you is perfect." She kissed his pec.

Josh could only make incoherent noises.

"How do you want this to be? Like this? Or under me?"

He blinked. "This." He was dangerously close already. "I'm sorry, I don't think it'll take much."

With a smile, she grabbed the box, watching him, and took a condom out. She glanced down at his cock with a raised brow.

"What? What's wrong?"

"You're just right."

"Really?" He peered down, his cock hard, and the pulse of pleasure intensified. It was hot, and all he wanted to do was be inside her.

"Yes." She reached down and grasped him.

Josh grunted and lifted his head back. The feel of her fingers made him harder, cock twitching in her hand. His arms began to shake. She kissed his shoulder and rolled it on. He couldn't draw breath. Her soft touches, and the strange sensation of cool latex, alien and new, reset his brain.

Bea pulled him down to her as she lay back, and Josh was greedy for her mouth. She angled her hips and legs so he was placed just right. He lifted his head, relishing the anticipation and hot fever in his desire. She smiled, caressing him, waiting. Touching his forehead to hers, his hair fell forward, and he eased in. Tight and hot and perfect.

He didn't know the strangled sound was him. She clenched around his cock, and he moved, instinct taking over. He went slowly, savouring every second.

Resting on his elbows, his hands cradling her head, fingers tangled in her hair, and he kissed her head.

Exquisite.

The feeling was so intense, he didn't process it but felt. He was all sensation, and Bea was beautiful and soft yet strong. He stared into her eyes and shook his head.

It was too much. He needed to make her come.

Josh bit the inside of his cheek and halted.

"What's wrong?"

"Trying not to come, I want you to first."

She chuckled. "I came pretty hard from you eating me."

"I need it."

With a nod, she shifted and stuttered a whisper. "Relax your stomach and take deep breaths."

He nodded, and she moved more, angling her hips up. He thrust again, and she put her hands on his bum, pinching him and guiding his movement. He went with it, deep and measured and kept breathing, trying not to be overwhelmed by how incredible it was.

Her lips were dark and her face flushed, and his orgasm hovered. Wetter with every movement, she moved with him, hot breathy moans, and when she got tighter, he shook, still thrusting, holding back, desperate for the spiralling want coiled in his muscles.

She lurched up until she pressed her face into his neck and came. The grip on his cock, the rush of warmth in her smooth heat was too intense, he bucked into her hard, balls tight, dick pulsing, and she thrust up to meet him.

"Yes, take it." Her strangled voice was all he needed, and he held tight and took her. His hips worked hard and fast, and Bea cried out as she pulled his hair. He came in an electric rush of pleasure, his cock pulsing, and the orgasm filled every nerve and muscle, pulling from somewhere deep.

His raspy growl as he came didn't signal how good it felt. No words could.

Letting his weight press on her, he twitched and shivered as pleasure shimmied through him. She still clenched, moaning under him.

It was the most perfect moment. Bea was his, no, he was hers. He would do anything for her. Anything. He loved her in his bones, and it was the truth of him. Emotion threatened, but he held it back.

"Are you all right?" she whispered into his neck.

Josh swallowed. His cock was still hard. "It was..." Revelatory? Pure? He nuzzled her cheek, too overwhelmed.

"Was what?" Her heart pounded.

"Beautiful." He felt her smile against him as she squeezed him in her embrace.

For a second, he savoured it, and he smoothed back her hair, their breathing calming. He pulled out, worried he was crushing her and frowned at the cum-filled thing on his cock. She took it off and put it in the wrapper. He smiled in a daze while they arranged themselves under the blankets so she was the little spoon as they lay side on. He smoothed her hair and could live the rest of his life like that.

A flamed curled over the log, rippling red. Josh took a deep breath as she snuggled into him. He kissed her hair, and she hummed. A rare, weird ease that he rarely felt around others bloomed in him. Everything relaxed.

It was nice that they barely needed words. What Bea gave him was beautiful, and emotion pulled at him like a thread, but his inclination as always was to pull it. To unravel it. But he didn't. He held on and wound it around him, holding her tight.

Then he remembered it would all end. They would clear the snow. He'd do what was needed, and she'd be gone from his life. Josh wanted to hold onto her and keep her close. But she had to go back to Chadford, back to the reality of her situation. He couldn't go with her. Anything, he thought only a minute ago, he'd do anything for her. That included letting her go because he couldn't give her what she needed.

Josh, the protector and strength that kept her safe. He wasn't those things anymore if he ever was.

He let a fantasy play out in his mind where they stayed together.

The log popped and fell apart.

Embers

Bea leant into his hold. The man had a gift for turning her on with his words, and she was beyond relieved that it was the same in person.

She was calm and satisfied. Josh's arm grew heavy, and she smiled. With a yawn, she nestled into him. The wind howled outside, and the chaos and bad weather raged around their perfect calm. In a few days, they'd leave, and she didn't know what waited for her. The fear of the people after her crawled up her throat. She shut it out. For now, they had this, and it needed to be enough.

She should get him to speak to Denbridge so they knew. She should do a lot of things.

But a pit of worry in her stomach kept turning. She'd lose him. The doubt needled. Yet she hoped.

She woke before dawn, stretching under the man half-lying on top of her. Her back was stiff, and the air frigid. Bob was nestled up close to them and under the covers. She fussed him.

Bea nudged Josh, and he opened his eyes.

"Fucking hell, it's cold." He was adorably grumpy.

She fished about for her clothes, pulled them on and cleared and remade the fire. Ash scattered on the tiles. She was stiff and sore, but her pain wasn't too bad, though her eye pulsed sharply.

"I'll clean up when it's warmer," he muttered.

Sun crept under the curtains, and she opened them, wincing at the light. A crisp, bright yellow dawn greeted them. The land was thick and white, sun reflecting off, sky clear blue, and air still.

She shivered. Her body hurt, head too, but despite everything, she was calm.

Josh stood behind and held her, resting his chin on her shoulder.

"It's beautiful."

"It is," he said as he pecked her neck. "How do you feel?"

"Stiff. It's bright."

Josh smoothed her hair and put his hand over her eye. "There. Coffee, proper breakfast, then we move snow so we can heat the water. I'll find you some painkillers."

"Okay."

Neither moved but gazed out at the snow. Bob startled them into action by barking to go out.

A full veggie fry-up and a vat of coffee later, Bea was bundled up in several layers and a coat that was too big and waddled out the back door, wearing his sunglasses. The snow drifted more than two-foot up one side of the cottage, but it was to her shoulders at the front and garage side.

Josh had a large snow shovel in the utility and a spade. They — mostly Josh — dug a small trench, and Josh fetched the ladders and made his way up all the while Bob watched from the door porch in his checked fleecy dog coat, unsure of all the cold white. Bea stayed with him as thick sheets of snow fell, and she shovelled it out of the way, gritting her teeth through the strain.

Bea took a break, her breath puffing out as she pulled down the scarf. She sweated under her layers. The view was spectacular. Rolling hills blanketed in pristine white, trees like perfect lace, but where the village was, fear stabbed.

"You okay?" Josh called down.

"Will they be looking yet?"

He climbed down the ladder. "You think it's bad here? It'll be deeper there because it drifts. There will be no free roads in and out until they've manually dug this end, and a plough can move some on the way in. Plus, if they weren't prepared for the weather in their haste, they won't be able to explore on foot. These hills and banks are impassable now."

She nodded.

"When was the last time you had any fun?"

"Last night."

He laughed, offering a delightful smile. "I mean, just fun." He stepped away and made a snowball and threw it at her but missed. Bob barked and tried to eat it.

She limped a bit, using the shovel to support herself, made one, and managed to land it. Bob explored the deeper snow, jumped in and vanished, then jumped up and out again, giving a thorough shake and showered them in snow.

They both laughed, and she fussed him, putting the shovel aside, and holding his collar as she walked. He went slowly and was tall enough to support her.

Josh's face grew soft and sad.

"Let's build a snowman." She eyed the pile of snow.

They rolled a chunk, pulling up more snow until it was waist-high, and it ended at the garden. They made a second and lifted it by rolling it up the lower half.

"Now what?" Josh panted.

"Um." She fussed Bob. "I don't know."

Josh went off, and she kept fussing Bob and bent down to kiss his muzzle. "Oh, your nose is so cold, baby, yes it is." The animal whined and snuffled.

Josh came back with lumps of concrete and branches. He gave one to Bob, who held it in his mouth like it was first prize in something. They put the others in as arms and the bits of rubble as eyes and a mouth.

Bea grinned, and for a moment, she forgot. Josh played tug with Bob and his branch, and Bea laughed. Warmth spread in her. This is how it should be. Could be if not for the world beyond. She was desperate to hold onto it.

"We should get back to work."

"Boo," she said to Bob in a baby voice.

Josh shook his head.

By lunch, the roof was clear, and they'd made a path to the front of the house.

Her back was sore and body stiff. Her neck and hips, especially.

"You okay?" Josh helped her take off the coat and boots.

"Yeah." Bea stretched her neck, and Josh massaged it. She melted into the gentle touch with a low moan.

He cleared his throat, his fingers lingering there. "How about some lunch while we wait for the water and have hot showers?"

"That sounds like heaven." Bea turned to him and wondered for a second how long she could draw out staying here.

He kissed her forehead, staying close by. Even sweaty and pink from the cold, he was alluringly sexy. Especially when he was sweaty. Her clit pulsed at the memory of him above her, the sounds he made, feel of his body and the look in his eyes. She swallowed the saliva in her mouth.

"Are you sure you're all right?"

"Yes, perfectly." She kissed the corner of his mouth and limped into the kitchen, holding onto Bob. She shivered as she stood at the range and put the kettle onto boil.

Bea got the mugs ready and saw him watching her. She raised her brows.

"I wanted to, um, hold you."

She grinned and reached out a hand.

Strong arms enveloped her from behind, and he kissed her neck. Patches of his face were stubbly and others rough, and she liked it. The reality was so much better than the fantasy.

"Bea."

She loved that gravelly sound. She hummed, and leaning back to his face, he kissed up her cheek. Turning in his hold, she kissed him, hard and needy, pulling on him.

"Fuck." He pulled away and held her shoulders. "I need a shower."

"Me too."

Bea could taste the tension, and it tasted like fresh sweat and bright winter sun.

"It'll be a couple of hours."

"We can wait."

"Uh-huh." Josh licked his lips and pressed her against the kitchen cabinets. He caged and overwhelmed her. It was perfect and not enough. He hovered too close and too far away, mouth tantalisingly near.

Bea brushed her face against his, waiting.

Josh laughed, a little-used action, but it was wonderful and broken. When he glanced down shyly, she cupped his face and kissed him. He hummed, lifting her onto the work surface and returned her need. Her legs pulled him closer. Their hands grabbed, trying to get more, his hard tongue in her mouth sought deeper, teeth caught, and lips bruised. She kissed him like the world was ending until the kettle whistled, and Bea jumped a foot in the air.

Josh slid it off the heat, still looking at her, panting hard. "Tea."

Skimming her thighs with his fingertips, he left her hold, and she wanted him back there. After sandwiches and soup for lunch with mugs of tea, Bea was shattered. Josh tidied up while she closed her eyes at the table, light stabbing through her lids. Bob put his head on her knee and whined, and Bea absently stroked his head until she drifted off. Josh gently woke her, taking her hand and leading her upstairs. The cold woke her up, and upstairs was possibly as frigid as outside.

"Why don't you have heating?" she slurred.

"Ah, well, no gas up this way, and I don't want tanks. I'm having ground source as well as underground air. Are you all right?"

"Nerve pain."

He frowned. "Come on."

He hoisted her up in his arms with a grunt, and she buried her face in his neck. After he set her on the bed, he closed the curtains. Not to be left out, Bob jumped on the bed and lay next to her.

"It's okay." Josh soothed her forehead when he joined them, and she held his hand to her eyes, shutting all light out. They curled up together, and he stroked her brow with his thumb. He was warm and safe, and so was she.

A while later, she came to, her head pounding.

"I can help you shower."

"Sounds nice. Not hair, though." She clung tighter to him.

He went through the vanity and found a hairband and tied her hair up. He stripped her quickly, her skin goosing and stripped himself as the water heated and steamed. They hugged under the cascade of water and warmed before washing each other down as she tried to keep her hair dry. It felt good to be warm and clean. The water cooled, and they got out. She cleaned her teeth, sat on the closed toilet while he shaved by feel.

She guessed it wasn't that much different from her shaving her armpits and pubes. She'd wrapped up in a big towel but still shivered. Josh rubbed his hair dry and picked her up. She giggled and laughed, and he urged her into bed.

Josh made Bob lie in his bed by the heater and slid in with Bea. She slept for a while, needing rest, and woke with a stretch. Josh was stroking her hair.

"Hey." He smiled and kissed her forehead.

"When are we?"

"You've been asleep a few hours." The light was still bright but wan, paling as the clear sun faded.

Bea kissed his neck. She felt the hard length of him press into her. "Someone is awake."

"I don't seem to be able to will it away near you."

She laughed. "I can help you with that."

"You don't need to."

"I want to. Lie back." She ran her tongue down his chest to the outline of abs, along his scars and strip of hair. She parted his thighs, feeling up and down the muscle, strong and firm. The scent of his skin and the tremor of his body lured her down until her cheek brushed his cock, and he half sat up with a cry.

"No, you should rest."

"How about a lazy blow job?" She pecked his thigh, the muscle twitching.

Josh tensed. "But your head."

"Has eased." She ran her tongue along the inside of the firm line of his thigh. "It's been so long since I've done this. I want it. But only if you do." Bea's lips were parted, and she stared at his thick, not-too-long-but-long-enough dick.

He breathed hard, a ragged sound interrupted by a loud swallow. "Please."

"Please what?"

"Put me in your mouth."

She licked from base to shaft, and he swore. Bea sucked him slow and as deep as she could, hand around his shaft, resting her head on her other hand. He was hot, and the clean scent of him warmed her senses, her lips stretched, tongue sliding and swirling around him, and Josh was rigidly still.

As he relaxed, remembering to breathe, he slipped his hands over her shoulders, and his hips moved. She laughed as he bent a knee up and hissed.

"You have to stop so I don't come in your mouth."

She didn't.

She worked harder, pressing the tip of her tongue up and down the ridged underside of his cock, and pulse of his need was vulnerable and perfect. The needy sounds he made and twitchy thighs let her know he was close.

"Bea." She barely understood the word. "I'm coming."

He gripped her shoulders, cried in a breath and came. Tangy cum filled her mouth. It was always a touch jarring, but she didn't care, she just wanted him. She kept going, slower, bringing him down, taking it all and sucked him clean until he squirmed.

She let him go and resting her head on his stomach, feeling his heart pound.

"Fuck."

"Give yourself a second first."

He laughed and ran his fingers through her hair, winding and separating the curls.

"Did you like that?"

"Yes. But because you gave it. You know?" He wrapped his thighs around her, his cold feet crossing around her bottom.

"I get it." She snuggled in. "This is nice."

"This is everything I ever hoped. It's perfect."

She didn't know what to say. It was true. She climbed up and curled over him. "Am I too heavy?"

"No, just right."

"Can I stay here with you?"

"Bea..."

"I know. I know. Let's pretend for a while."

He didn't speak at first. "I have a plan. We need to leave before they're able to find you. I'm the only place out here. Get a car. Chadford."

"Back to Denbridge," she whispered.

"They can protect you."

"Can't we try?"

Josh rocked her. He sighed deeply as their foreheads touched.

He stroked her cheek, frowning. "I was protecting a woman, and there was a fire."

"Was she okay?"

"Yes." He blinked a few times and sagged. "Then I was protecting Matt's girlfriend, and I was attacked." He clutched her face in his hands, eyes almost wild. "I'm not okay. I haven't been for a long time, and I want to be."

Bea chewed the inside of her lip.

"I was homeless. Shit life, and then I met Edie and Sid, and they saved me. I had this whole need to help others because I couldn't help myself as a kid. So Sid knew a guy, and I got into personal security, seemed a good fit. I was a quiet kid, but people seemed to be intimidated by me. Anyway, I was young and reckless and thought I was invincible. After the fire... I lost hope. But Edie and Sid never doubted me. They saved my life as much as CAPTA. That's how I met Matt. He was running a recruitment thing there, they do events because it used to be mostly military. He took me on. I was silent and angry. I didn't go back into personal security, just investigation and observation. Even that was too much. It ate me up. After I got my arse kicked, I was done.

"Sometimes we cling to the things that we thought were part of us, and I didn't know who I'd be without that. I've found other paths. New peace. I never thought I'd find it." He cupped her cheek. "You're the right person."

"Wrong time," she mumbled. Bea understood, and it hurt her heart.

His chin trembled, and he turned away. "I will help you, I swear. I don't know if I can be what you want me to be, and that's not because of you."

"Then we have this. And I will cherish it no matter what happens."

He kissed the tears from her cheeks she couldn't hold in and then devoured her mouth, and she gave back, rolling them onto his back. He grabbed a condom from his sweats nearby, offered a smile at her raised brow as he rejoined her.

"Fuck, I'm so sensitive." He arched back.

"Let me." She straddled him, her hips not too stiff.

She sheathed him when he nodded, jaw twitching. She entwined her fingers with his, easing onto his dick. He watched with adoration as she rode him but held her hips to help her move. Inching up and down with the duvet over her shoulders.

His mouth opened in bliss, not in frenzied need, but slow and sweet, though intensity wound through her body. She met his eye, demanding he stay with her, and for a few minutes he did, but his thighs tensed, and he sat up. Hands cupped her bottom, and she ground deeper and slower. He grunted with each circle of her hips, the wet grind rubbing delightfully on her clit, he kissed her shoulder, and she grasped his lush and thick hair in her fingers. The silent connection deepened in building desire. She could stay her whole with him that way.

She didn't hold back. Unabashed and loud, she took what she wanted.

"Bea."

She searched his eyes, and his face filled with wonder. Her head pitched back as she came, her muscles tight, and she fucked him, and the duvet fell away.

"Yes." He squeezed her arse and supported her as each wave of intense pleasure rolled through her body. His grunts joined her cries, and he thrust up to her as she fell on him, limp, relishing Josh squeezing tight and losing himself, thrusting up hard, and fuck, she needed him to take her until he stilled, cock pulsing inside her.

He flopped back, and she went with him, pulling the cover back over them to keep them warm.

"Oh fuck," he panted.

Bea was done in, and in the moments when she caught her breath, knowing this would end, she'd leave a part of her with him. He already had it.

Dying Light

Josh watched Bea play with Bob. It was early, and after a night of gentle desire and exploration, he wasn't sure about anything anymore. How she led him, how she wrung his lust from him like a bell. It was loud and reverberated through him. But there was no taking of anything he wasn't prepared to give. It was gentle and loving. She was the softest caress.

She'd told him more than once about what she desired. The prospect of falling into it lay before him. He could have it.

He nearly smiled at the sight before him, but the ache in his heart tugged. It was almost time. They'd be digging the village out already.

His phone vibrated on the kitchen side, and it was Sid.

"Wondered how you were getting on."

"Fine." Josh didn't take his eyes off Bea. "I'm going to need some help. How bad is it?"

"Oh bad. Gritters can't get up, and the power went. But it's on now, and we're digging as a group. There was a to-do though the other day. Someone went missing."

"Pop. She's here, but don't tell anyone. We're going to make our way to you, and I need a truck. There'll be no way I can get mine out."

Sid didn't answer right away. "What's going on?"

"She's a Denbridge client. It's her. The woman I told you about." His voice broke, and he cleared it.

"Then don't come here, make your way up to the lot. There's a silver pickup that works, but the rest are being stripped. Keys are in the safe. It's taxed and insured. I was going to use it instead of the van now for work."

The lot was for the overspill of the yard and was on the far side of the pasture.

"Thank you. Let me know when the main road is passable."

"Right. Be careful, son."

"You too. Love to Edie."

"Aye."

It was a better plan.

Bea looked up from Bob, who was at her mercy, on his back, and happier than any creature had the right to be. Part of him envied that state of being.

"What's going on?" Bea asked, her gentle voice quiet.

"Finalising the plan."

"We're going?"

"When Sid tells me."

She didn't answer, and Josh pottered, made them coffee and let Bob out to wee in the patch of ground they'd cleared for him, and he came back in as soon as he could.

"Tell me about them," She asked, blowing on her cup when he sat with her.

"They found me sleeping behind their car dealership and garage when they had it in Chadford. They fed me, offered me their home in exchange for helping out around the house. They never had kids and were older. They're good people. Edie's from here, and when they retired, they sold up and came back."

"You stayed in the city."

He nodded as he picked up his mug and sipped it. "First time I came up to visit her family when I was still a teen, it was like coming home. It was always the plan. Then the fire happened."

"I'm sorry you went through it."

He nodded. "Being here helps me. I can't be in the city, I can't go back to that life. I-"

"I know." So much regret in those two words. She didn't meet his eyes and reached over, squeezing his wrist. Too much unsaid.

"Bea," he whispered, pain throbbing in his chest.

"Can I..."

"What?"

Bea set her mug down and then his. "Comfort you?"

"Comfort?"

"Hold you. Soothe you. Whatever you want it to be."

He let a long breath go, flushing and kissed her. A soft, gentle kiss, but it was hard not to be swept away by her. He held her tight and, pulling close, deepened the kiss until his need overcame him to keep her close. She could stay, couldn't she? Why not? But he knew the answer. He knew.

She urged him down in front of the fire, and he lost himself in her kiss. Pulling away, he gazed at her lips. "I want you."

Bea turned over and reached for the condoms. She peered back over her shoulder, holding one up.

He pulled up her top and kissed her back.

Bea gasped, and he took the foil wrapper from her fingers before pulling off her bottoms. The mix of cold and warmth from the fire made him shiver as he moved about behind her. She pulled a pillow under her stomach, and he parted her legs, lying over her back, elbows either side of her head, and she rested it to the side.

"This okay?"

"Perfect." She lifted her bottom, and he fumbled, hands shaking as he eased into her.

Her smile faded as he slid deep, lying down, pinning her with his body and letting out a raspy grunt. He moved agonisingly slow.

Josh shifted one arm across her front, and she rested her chin on it, so he angled deeper. Bea moaned, their faces side by side, his weight keeping her still, and breath soft as he undulated his hips into her.

"Am I too heavy?"

"No." She could barely speak and not move at all.

"Talk to me," he said against her cheek.

She kissed his forearm — it was about as much as she was able to do — and moaned.

"More, harder. Slower." She hissed. "Angle up. There."

He obeyed her direction, needing to show her how much she meant, and give her what he could in that moment. She needed more, and he thrust harder, letting go of his hesitation. Free with her to be something he'd never been or would again as he flexed as deep as he could, holding before jolting into her. His body strained at the effort.

"Josh... don't stop, I'm..." Her eyes widened before narrowing, and a long, deep cry came out of her. Tensing then relaxing, her body under him was divine, and he was fascinated by her responses. All the while, he undulated slower and slower until her pussy squeezed his cock in long, hard spasms. She hitched her breaths between the sweetest sounds of pleasure.

"I love making you come," he kissed her cheek.

Just when he thought she might pass out, he eased up, one hand on her shoulder and one supporting his weight as he shifted his legs.

"Yes?"

"Please." She made desperate noises, grasping his arm.

Then he fucked her. Hard and fast. It was deep and unrelenting and perfect.

She cried out, egging him on, holding his wrist and the pillow in front of her, riding out the most intense orgasm he'd experienced until he stilled before a final thrust. He poured himself into her, needing to give her everything.

He growled his breath as he rested down on her and pressed kisses everywhere he could reach until she squirmed and laughed.

"You're incredible," he panted.

"I just lay here."

"Sorry-"

"It was amazing." She stuttered in a giggle.

He withdrew and dealt with the thing on his dick while she closed her eyes. He redressed her, and after she went to the loo, got them comfy. There was nowhere he'd rather be than with her in his arms right then. Bob joined them and flopped down by Bea with a gruff sigh as if sensing it was safe. Her breathing changed, and contentment washed over them, uncertainty fading away.

He nestled close and kissed the back of her head. He wasn't sure how he could let her go.

"Bea," he barely whispered it, but she didn't move. "I love you."

Her steady breathing told him she was asleep, and that was probably for the best.

∞ ∞ ∞

It was bright when Josh opened his eyes. Time and days lost meaning for him after a while, but every waking second with her was precious.

He watched her sleep. She was exhausted. A single wily curl fell over her face, and he smoothed it back.

He got up, desperate for the loo.

Sharp sun lit the snowy landscape, and though the air was bitter, the wind was still. The world was silent.

A message from Sid said they were close to clearing the road. It wasn't even midday.

It was time.

He fed Bob, washed up and changed and went down and got the range going. Bea sat up, bleary, and her hair standing on end on one side.

"Huh?" She yawned.

"Hey." He made her a coffee and toast and took it over, kissing her head.

She sipped it as he cleaned and relit the fire. The scent of ash and smoke clung to the room, and he tuned it out.

"We should start digging our way out today."

"Already?" Her voice was flat, and she blew on the hot drink as she clung to it.

He closed the stove door, watching the fire take through the glass. "We can't wait any longer and have to get you out of here. We agreed." He regretted the words and harsh tone instantly and wanted to take it back. He cleared his throat and turned.

Bea stared at him, her face blank before she stood and left. He sighed and tidied up.

She came back in her jeans and top, boots in hand, and wore a pair of his socks.

"I'm sorry."

She ate her cold toast. "It's okay."

"Bea, it came out wrong."

"No, you're right, we agreed."

There was so much he wanted to say, but he just nodded, gripping the back of the chair. It was different speaking in person, and at least with texts, he had time to consider what he said, but he blurted everything out wrong with her there.

They worked quietly and dug as they did before. The bright, bitter day was only broken by the sound of them working, Bob playing in the snow, and Josh was soon sweating. They halted for tea, and her nose was pink and eyes hidden by his sunglasses as she sipped from her thermos cup.

"Bea, I don't want this to be awkward, and I'm sorry I can't do or say the right thing."

She nodded, tapping the snow shovel against her foot, jaw set and shrugged him off.

"Bea, please."

"It's harder than I expected. I'm afraid. In pain. You were the only thing that gave me hope."

"We can still talk and text." He didn't understand the look on her face.

"You think we can go back?" she asked.

"Can't we?"

She cleared her throat. "Can you? I want to be with you, and you're telling me never. That's your right, there's no obligation, and you shouldn't do anything you don't want. But there are consequences to that. I can't be torn into hoping and waiting for a thing you tell me can't happen." Her voice faded into nothing.

He took the cup and pulled her to him, their foreheads touching. The hood of his coat fell back from her face, and he kissed her.

Tears filled his eyes. "This is heaven and agony. We have everything, but it's going to be over any moment, and I want to hold on, but the pain of waiting for it is–" He stopped abruptly, mouth hovering, their breaths misting. He didn't say anything, the words stuck in his throat, and she pulled away.

"Then let's get on with it."

Something precious withdrew between them. The danger of it made him shake. He wanted to hold on and love her the way she deserved.

Josh went inside, shed his outdoor gear, and tidied through, ensuring everything in the house was secure. He grabbed a holdall from his wardrobe and packed it. He felt nothing the whole time. Bea was sat on the bottom stair, muffling her tears when he stood on the landing.

"I never expected this. It's not something I thought would happen to me. I don't know what I'm doing. I'm not good for people."

Bea didn't turn. She wiped her cheeks and eased to her feet, massaging her hip. "It's okay, really." Her tone was shut down.

Josh couldn't blame her. He'd offered her everything and took it away again. He could list all the reasons over and over, but it wouldn't matter.

He finished getting ready and locked up, hating leaving, hating having to go back. She would never understand it, nor did he want her to really; he'd never wish how he felt on anyone.

Bea's presence tore him, and the pain in his chest brought tears to his eyes. He blinked them back as they went out into the cold, and he set the alarm. He whistled, and Bob came to heel.

With a longing glance at her, putting on his sunglasses, he put away the pain in his heart and focused.

Evasion

Bea took a deep breath of sharp, cold air. It was dry in her throat and numbed her face. She followed behind Josh, Bob right beside her as she clung to his lead.

She looked back at the cottage, knowing she was leaving one of the happiest times of her life. The bittersweet tug in her heart was already an ache.

Josh had a large holdall across his back, and she held onto the small handle with her free hand. They waded through the snow down an embankment that led to the trees. It was hard going. She walked into him when he came to a stop.

He clicked his fingers, and Bob went still. They'd halted at a hedgerow that skirted a small copse. Then she heard it.

The man climbed through the trees in the distance, wading noisily through the snow and hidden bracken. Bea held her breath, convinced he could hear her heart pounding. The world froze, and she started to sweat hard. Josh moved to a crouch, and she followed. Bob whined.

"Stay low." He eased the holdall off and slid out a short baton from the side pocket. He was deathly still, but when he glanced at her, he was livid.

Mute in her terror, she nearly reached for him, but he stalked off into the trees, extending the baton.

Bea clung to bob in a painful crouch and only heard a few muffled cries and thumps. Then a few minutes of nothing, and her mind raged in panic.

Josh hurried back, throwing the holdall over his shoulder again. "Go."

They went in complete silence; only the sounds were their coats and breath, which echoed in her ears. At the bottom, the snow was deeper but disturbed. Josh helped her over the fence and urged her to wait secluded with the dog.

"I'll check the room."

She nodded and gave him the key. It had been the only thing she'd had on her when josh found her. He left the bag with her, rubbed the dog's head and moved off. He sidled the back of the pub, peeking around the corner for a minute, and went in quickly. The light was failing already. Bea had no idea what time it was or what day it was. She'd lost all perspective. Bob whined, and she soothed him as much as possible.

The seconds crawled past, and she kept looking about. The SUV was still parked in the car park. A wave of bitter anger filled her blood. In the bag was a multitool; she'd seen Josh slide in it. She found it, turned the stiff handles out, and it opened into gripped pliers. With Bob staying close, they went to the vehicle, and she uncapped the first tire, and holding the pliers, squeezed the air inlet. Air rushed out. She did the next, her arms straining at the effort.

It couldn't have been more than five minutes but felt like hours when Josh returned with her bags. He smirked at her and jerked his head. "Let's go." He carried everything, and they hurried along the hedgerow until they turned off onto a private road that skirted a pasture filled with chickens. On the other side were the garage and a bungalow. Bob went on the alert and wuffed, and a little brown chicken clucked and barrelled up to the fence. Patches of snow lay in piles that the chickens pecked around.

"Bob, leave her."

"That's the chicken you told me about?" It was tiny.

"Barbara, the chicken, is the antichrist, don't be fooled. Bob is onto her."

Bea repressed the bubble of laughter and focused. She wanted to cry and scream and laugh hysterically.

There was an old lockup with car parts dotted about, all covered in snow. Inside the patched building were a couple of cars and one faded silver pickup. At the far side was a tiny office, and Josh spent a few minutes searching for keys and came out, just as they heard steps crunching through the snow.

A large man in a thick wool coat and fleecy hat appeared. "Well. You found them."

Bob whined, and the man fussed him.

"Sid, this is Bea."

"Oh aye. Nice to meet you."

She shook Sid's gloved hand. "Hello."

"You want me to have the dog?"

"It might be best." Josh squatted. "Don't start shit with Barbara. You can't finish it." He kissed the top of the dog's head and stroked him. "Thanks, Pop."

Bea fussed and whispered love and silliness to the animal, and he whined, giving her the saddest expression.

"I saw someone lurking about. Called Phil." Sid took the dog lead.

"Who's Phil?" Bea asked.

"Copper. He lives here."

Bea swallowed and stepped back.

"He's all right. You can trust him."

"What did you say?" Josh asked.

"Just that they were dodgy. Pointed them out when we were clearing the main road."

"Thanks. You can tell him the SUV was used in an attempted murder. It needs checking for repairs. The bastard was heading up to my place when we left. I think I slowed him down a bit. We best get going before Phil wants to talk to us."

Bob yipped and gave Josh his best distressed puppy eyes.

Josh urged Bea into the car. It smelt musty and old.

"Don't worry, Edie will do nothing but feed him, and he'll forget I exist." Josh started the car, waved and set off.

They went slowly. The roads were slippy, even where they were clear, but they were wet and ice-free when they got to the A-roads, with mounds of dirty snow banked at the sides.

"Are we going to talk about what you did to that guy?" Her vision vibrated with the question.

He sighed, focused on the road. "Beat the living fuck out of him with a baton and stole his keys and wallet."

Bea stared.

"He was going to kill you, right? Probably the one who ran you off the road. Fucker is lucky I didn't kill him." His voice was gravelled fire.

With a swallow, she nodded slowly. "Thanks." She didn't know how she felt about being so close to the man who'd come to finish what he started, Josh battering him, or that they just left him there to go about his business.

Shuddering, Bea closed her eyes while the world moved too quickly. She relived every touch between them. It wasn't enough. She needed more.

They stopped at a petrol station, and Bea stretched. She missed her crutch. The car park was nearly empty except for a few lorries, vans, and the occasional car. The quiet was unnerving and air bitter. Josh came back with a bag of snacks. Neither spoke.

The further south they headed, the lighter the snow was, and it was the middle of the night by the time they reached Greater Chadford.

Tension and awkwardness increased as they left the motorway.

They pulled into a big chain hotel car park, and weary, checked in.

At the reception, he slid over a card and said, "It's for a client."

The receptionist's eyes widened, and she typed furiously and gave a sharp nod as she passed over the key cards.

Josh paid cash, and she expected them to have separate rooms. She was surprised when he led them into the room, slotting the key card into the electric switch and turned on the lights.

Bea stood in front of the bathroom mirror for a minute in the buzzing quiet. This was it. They had one more night.

She washed her face, wincing at the light.

Bea found him perched on the end of the bed, hands resting on his lap and his eyes closed.

He opened them and held her waist when she stood between his knees.

His fingers dug in, and Bea threw her head back so he wouldn't see her cry. He rested his face against her stomach.

"Don't leave me." She ran her hands through his hair. "Please don't leave me alone." She knew he'd say no before she said it, but she needed to fight for them and would regret it if she didn't try.

"I can't stay here."

"Then let me stay with you. Matt can help, and then I can go back." Bea didn't believe her own words as she said them. She couldn't go back or put him in further danger after what he'd done for her already. She couldn't cause him any more pain. Her heart hammered in the silence, and she felt him thinking as he held still. The dark part of him, the part he needed to get rid of, had to be present for him to help her; she'd seen it when he stopped the man after her. Bea understood. Letting him go was impossible.

"We can't."

"I'm not ready for it to end." Her voice shook, eyes filling with tears.

"Listen to me." He leant back, but she wouldn't lift her eyes. "When it was texts and calls, it was different, and I thought maybe I could, but I can't give you what you need."

Bea lost the fight with holding back the tears, and they came as she nodded. She pulled away and turned from him, staring out the hotel window past the light snow to the city where sparkling yellow light glittered through the dark, and with a blister of frustration, she hobbled to the door and opened it. Josh appeared behind her and slammed it shut. Bea put both her hands on the door, and he held her waist.

"Don't think I want this to end." His breath whispered on her neck. "I want you. I want to be with you. Bea." He kissed the skin his lips brushed.

"Then be with me." The words twisted.

"I'm not ready."

"I know. I know." And she'd pushed. Hoped. Needed him, never mind what he needed. She was selfish and callous and hated herself for hurting him and bringing him into her mess.

More hot tears fell as she sagged in his embrace, savouring that last one. The last time she'd cling to the hope he gave her. "Go."

"Bea."

"I don't think I can bear a night of being with you but not with you. It hurts too much. It's best if I'm alone." It wasn't. She wanted to make love to him, but it was wrong.

"I'm sorry."

"Don't be. I understand." Her flat voice gave nothing away as her heart broke in two when he moved away from the door.

His chin trembled.

Bea felt fragile and small when she faced him. "Goodbye, Josh."

Tilting his head back, pain etched his face. He went to her, cupped her face, and pressed a kiss to her lips. "I love you."

Her face twisted, eyes filling with tears again. "I love you too. I wish it was enough." A tear fell, and she pulled away.

When the door closed behind him, she needed him to come back and hold her. Love her. Bea gave in, collapsing on the bed and sobbed until she passed out.

Freshly Fallen

Josh stood outside her door, trying to figure out how that had gone so wrong. As the shock wore off, he knew it was for the best. A clean break.

Closing his eyes, he rested his forehead on the frame, and his fist curled. The lift doors pinged down the corridor, bringing him back to himself, and he went to get a second room.

Alone, he went through the wallet. Cash, driving licence, credit card. He memorised the photo and the name. He took a deep breath, reliving what happened. His heart had pounded and was the only sound when he'd stalked through the wood. He came up behind him, striking with the baton in a sharp crack. The thug staggered, and Josh had struck three more times before they grappled, and he took the man in a headlock, squeezing until he passed out. The violence vibrated in him. He was there to kill her. The idea terrified him. He could've easily ended them him then. He wouldn't. That wasn't who he was.

He'd also taken the pocketknife he had on him, an ugly thing with a sharp blade.

Josh's face crumpled, and he sobbed, but it turned into a growled cry. The anguish in his heart tore through his body in a white-hot fury. He needed to hold Bea, keep her safe and shield her from terror. With gritted teeth and a shuddering breath, he pressed the palms of his hands to his eyes. No, this was the right thing to do. How else was she expected to react? She was under immense stress, had trauma, and he'd taken away their connection.

It would be so easy to go to her, kneel and beg for her love to soothe him like a balm. But it wasn't right. It'd be a projection and distraction and would only hurt her more in the end.

Calmer, Josh texted Matt, and they made a plan.

In the morning, she met him in reception, and they went for breakfast. She didn't speak.

Josh had no appetite and sipped juice. "I'm sorry. That's not how I meant for it to go."

"I know. It doesn't matter now," Bea stuttered. Her eyes were swollen, she was pale and unable to look at him.

There was a new coldness to her. Detached. He'd done that. "Are you okay?"

"In pain. Didn't sleep." She slid on his sunglasses.

After checking out, they drove into the city and to her flat.

A woman opened the flat door, salt and pepper short curly hair and the same eyes. She burst into tears and enveloped Bea.

She smoothed Bea's hair. "Why didn't you call me?"

Bea didn't answer.

"I'm Paula." She smiled politely, and they went in.

He set the bags down just as the door buzzer went. Selina appeared at the screen, and Paula let her in.

Sel gave Josh a knowing smirk, and he slumped against the wall.

"Had a fun little jolly?" Selina asked Bea.

Bea glanced at him. Josh folded his arms.

"Thank you for your help." She didn't answer Sel but raised her chin as she faced him.

He clenched everything, and consciously made himself relax. "Bea, I..."

They stared at each other.

A crushing weariness unfolded under his skin. He felt so heavy, he wanted to lie on the floor. Instead, he opened the door and left without another word.

In the cold, stark hallway, he froze. Unable to leave her. He couldn't do it. Breathing hard, panic filtered into him. He wanted to rage and scream and fight.

In a sudden flurry of making himself do something, he stormed down the stairs, forcing himself to go. For it to be done.

∞ ∞ ∞

Josh waited in Matt's office. Mira had hugged him and bustled off.

Matt shut the door and sat behind his immaculate desk. "He's been arrested." He took the bag Josh slid over of the things Josh confiscated.

"On what charge?"

"Trespassing. He was lurking around your home, trying to get in when the police went to check on your cottage. It's not much, but it means he can be held for questioning in connection to Bennet and the attempted murder of Bea."

Cold anger sliced through him. "She never really told me what happened."

"He ran her off the road to try and kill her. It was a miracle she survived at all. It was a terrible crash. The car rolled down an embankment, and she was trapped for a few hours as they tried to get her out. That she's recovered this much is impressive. It's all moving forward." Matt stared at him. "Selina said things were frosty."

Josh felt sick. He needed to hold her close. She'd suffered so much. "I can't give her what she needs. People don't fix their failings by falling in love."

Matt scowled. "No, they don't. But people find comfort and happiness in others. We're social animals and need people to some degree. They help us see ourselves, our worth, our flaws. The relationships we have give us a context of self. Support, strength and love. They can give us the tools we need to help ourselves."

"I have Sid and Edie."

"I have Willow, my mum and nan, my dad's big family in Canada, my circle of friends, my work colleagues, to name a few. They give me balance."

Josh shifted. "I'm consumed by her. This intensity can't be healthy. I need therapy and space and quiet. You know, when you put that docket in front of me, and I quit... I wondered what that said about me. About my failings. Who I am. She gave me perspective. I understand now. This is the right thing."

"Okay, but don't throw it all away because you're afraid."

"I have to go."

Matt tried to say more, but Josh had no patience to hear it. All he wanted to do was go home. Every mile he drove away from her hurt more than he imagined it could yet the solace of home called him back. Josh was hollow and numb, and he thought it was probably best that way.

He collected Bob, tired and weary when he got back to Deerbank, but Sid sat him down in the kitchen and put a pot of tea on.

"Tell me."

Josh told him about her.

Sid poured them a second cup. "Phil found him at the cottage, looking in through the windows. Arrested him. He had another bobby with him, just to make sure he complied. Well, he was taken down the nick and picked up from there. That great ugly car with the flat tires was seized. Not in the chap's name, apparently." Sid raised his brows. "There was a big to-do because the fella had been robbed, so he said, and had no ID, so took them a bit to sort the mess out, but a couple of bobbies took him off in the early hours." Sid picked up his mug in silence.

A sad, empty ache surfaced. He'd tried to keep it at bay, but it kept coming back. "Thank you."

"She seemed nice. Be good for you."

"Maybe."

Sid had a way of saying everything with few words. "I see." He sipped his drink, face wrinkled in concentration.

The cottage was cold and dark. He saw her on every surface, smelt her, felt her hair between his fingers. Bob followed him upstairs to bed, but it was worse. Every second of being with her crowded his mind until it was unbearable. He nestled into the spot where she'd lain. He could taste her. Scrubbing his face, he sat up. He'd neglected the group and idled the time by replying to messages. He went through her posts and photos.

He wasn't sure how he was going to be without her.

A week later, the snow had finally thawed properly. Josh went back to fixing fences and guttering and all the other things that went neglected.

He was painting the window frames at Sid and Edie's when his phone rang.

Selina.

Josh pulled off his work gloves. "Hi."

"You just fucked off then."

"What else was I meant to do?"

"Fight for her. She misses you."

He scrunched his face up and watched Bob watching Barbara. The pain was too intense. "I can't talk about it."

"Why?"

"Too painful."

"The CPS is moving forward, apparently. Long fucking list of charges."

He grunted an affirmation.

"She might have to testify."

He leant against the wall. "I don't know what I'm supposed to do about that."

"She'll need help."

"I can't help her. What help could I possibly be?"

"You're a fucking prick," She bit at him.

"I am. But it's a kindness. I'm no good."

"Not if you're like this. I thought you cared about her."

"Have to go." Tears cut off his voice, and he covered his eyes. Edie was watching him.

Josh got back to work.

His first therapy session was that afternoon. It'd been so long, and he didn't know where to start. His childhood? Bea? The fire?

His jaw twitched the whole time, tense and uncomfortable. He wasn't sure they'd be a good fit, but he had to try. The guy tried to push meds onto him, and he knew that wasn't his path. He just needed to unpack the past. By the end of the session, they both had an idea for a plan, and he'd give it a chance.

Restless and angry when he left, he took Bob for a run. He wore his thermal gear, and the dog lolloped along beside him as they climbed the hill trail. It was grey and bitter, and when he could no longer feel his face or hands, he stopped, stretching out.

Josh held the hair that escaped his beanie and pushed it back under. The view was clouded with hovering rain as the wind battered him. He closed his eyes, feeling Bea with him, and the pain washed through him.

It peaked in a sharp cut, and he bent over, growling at himself. He needed to gain control, detach and centre himself.

Bob whined.

"Come, boy." He turned from the sprawling view and slow jogged back. He didn't feel the tears as they fell.

Defence and Lies

Bea mooched through the collection of walking canes in the mobility centre and didn't like any of them.

"Well?" her mother offered.

"There all... old."

"What did you want?" Paula picked a flowery one out.

"I don't know. Something cool."

"We can try somewhere else."

"No." She picked out the only plain one.

An assistant wandered over. "We have a custom range from a local designer and only just got them in. We've been selling them online, they've done well, and I was about to set them out if you'd like to look?"

"Thank you."

She chose a neon blue one with an ergonomic black handle, sleek and lightweight, adjustable wrist chain, and pin-straight. It was twice as expensive as the others, but she loved it.

The assistant adjusted the height after she paid.

"Happy?"

"Yes." Her smile faded. She wanted to post to the group. She had a few messages asking where she was, but she didn't have the heart to reply. Josh still posted regularly.

It hurt too much to see him. She couldn't stop thinking about those last moments when he told her he loved her. She knew. And she knew he'd break then, that he'd stay for her if she said the word. It was the hardest thing she'd ever done to let him go. Those pained amber-brown eyes, glistening with pain and love haunted her.

They grabbed some lunch, and Bea bought a new black wool coat. As they were paying, her phone rang.

"Can you come to the police station? Don't worry, it's okay." Sel had her work voice on, and fear clutched Bea's insides.

It'd been more than a week. She knew Bennet had been rearrested and charged with a lot but had no idea about the details.

They headed over, taking a cab, and Shah met them in the reception when they arrived.

Sel stayed nearby.

"We'd like to show you a few photos, to see if any of the people in them are familiar. Is that all right?"

Bea nodded and took off her sunglasses, squinting at the light. In the interview suite, Shah set out six photographs. All men, white, but she wasn't sure except for one.

"He looks like the man who I saw at my window in Deerbank. Maybe the one who ran me off the road. They're very alike."

She swallowed hard. The car had vibrated as it skidded. She knew she rolled, loud and crunching, then ringing silence. Shock. She felt nothing and tasted blood.

Bea had cracked an eye and saw him watching next to the big SUV at the top of the embankment at the strange angle she was pinned in. He lit a cigarette. She held her breath and didn't move. Her vision stuttered white, piercing light cut with electric pain. Then there was nothing.

She tapped the photo. "Him. Definitely. He smokes. He had a tattoo on his hand. He was close enough that I could see it."

"Okay. Good, thank you." She put the photos away. "Micky Bennet has been charged with several offences. He's due to appear in court next week when he'll plead. The officer that's involved in the complaint has been charged as well.

"The person we have in custody for the attempt on your life will hopefully be charged today. We expect him to be remanded because of the danger to you, okay?"

Bea slumped, letting the tension go that she hadn't realised was there and nodded. Paula held her.

"The officer is cooperating, and we're really hoping Bennet pleads. There's so much evidence in the case that it's not focused on you anymore. Other than getting a confession, this is the best position we hoped for."

Bea steadied herself.

The first person she wanted to tell was Josh.

∞ ∞ ∞

"Let's go out," Sel said before Bea said hello when she came to the flat.

"Oh?"

"Celebrate."

Bennet was going to plead guilty. Guilty. They'd seized his drugs, weapons, had forensic and financial evidence, a slew of witnesses, CCTV, and records all so strong that her testimony would've been a footnote. They even had evidence of the contract on her.

Guilty.

Bea was still in shock after the court liaison officer called her.

"Okay."

"Excellent. Be ready at seven."

She wore a short silk patterned dress and low ankle boots. She wasn't sure how to go clubbing with a cane, but she'd make it work.

It was still cold, but the air changed, and the stark bitter winter winds had lessened.

They snagged a table in a huge Victorian refurbished pub.

"So, how do you feel?"

Bea knew it was coming. She drank her wine faster than she ought and sighed, people-watching. "I don't feel anything."

"I think that's okay. When are you going to therapy?"

"Friday."

"Have you spoken to him?"

Bea cleared her throat, blushing. "Too late." She pressed her tongue to the roof of her mouth as she held her breath. The pain was starting to feel like indigestion.

Sel put her hand over her wrist. "It'll be okay."

"Maybe. It was so perfect. I've never been that happy, and it was only for a few days when I was terrified, but being with him was more than I ever hoped. Now it's over. He was always there with a kind word and sweetness. Maybe I projected my need for comfort onto him. I don't know. I just know I miss him." Bea covered her mouth, unable to speak.

"Come on, we need somewhere livelier."

It was after ten when they reached the club, all flashing lights and heavy beats.

They did cheap shots of obnoxious bright liquid that could have been paint stripper. At the bar, a guy stared at Bea, looking her up and down.

He leaned in, shouting. "What's wrong with you?" he slurred, weaving right in her face.

"What the fuck did you say?" Selina put her arm around Bea's waist. She was too shocked to speak. She knew it'd happen at some point, but it took her by surprise. Heat burnt and then fury.

"Nothing is wrong with me, the real question is what's wrong with you, fucko." Bea adjusted her grip on the cane, ready to batter him.

"You fuck-"

Selina put her hand over Bea's death grip, making her lower her arm. "Hey, Johnny big bollocks, if you wanna still be using your cock to have your thirty seconds of pleasure, I suggest you walk away." The sharp cockney cut to her voice carried, and a few people turned to watch. The drunk guy stared back, but she never wavered, still smiling, and stood dangerously still. He looked away, shrugging and muttering under his breath.

Bea let a slow breath go, and Selina ordered more drinks.

"You okay, sweetie?" Her voice was measured again, her sharpness gone.

Bea nodded. "I wanted to beat the shit out of him."

"But you didn't, and to think my boss said I needed to retake my conflict management course." She downed a shot. "Let's dance." She took Bea's hand and led her over.

The slow lyrics etched in pain over the grimy beat spoke to Bea, and she closed her eyes as the bass pulsed and synths buzzed.

Standing at the edge of the dancefloor, she felt Josh's hands on her waist as she moved, hips circling with hers. His mouth on her neck as she tightened her grip on her cane. Aware of her body, arousal flooding her, she opened her eyes and saw him in her mind, walking to her, pulling her hard against him. Tears filled her eyes, and with the lust came pain; the two inextricable whenever she thought of Josh.

Bea smiled, turning slowly, pulled into the crowd of dancers, swaying and feeling him close. When she opened her eyes, she froze. A man with long hair covering one side of his face, and still as death stood at the far side of the dancefloor facing her. Bodies moved around them, but time slowed, and it was just them.

Her heart stopped and started. Beating hard and fast, pink light strobed, and she lost sight of him. She weaved through the crowd, pushing past hot, sweaty people, but found nothing.

She turned in circles, panic turned to tears, but she held it back and went to the ladies. Bright sound and yellow light brought her back to reality as she pushed down the corridor to the toilets.

She shook as she ran her wrists under cold water at a sink.

Selina barrelled in. "Are you all right?"

"I thought I saw him, but it wasn't. Couldn't have been." Bea drew in a sharp breath as her chest constricted.

"Who?"

"Josh."

She slumped, relieved. "Come on, hungry?"

"No. I just wanna go home."

Bea scanned the club as they went back out, squinting through the dim place as the wall of sound hit her until lights strobed through the beat, and she saw nothing but drunk arseholes.

It cut her deep. Did she imagine things? She tipped her head back to the chilly air outside, sweat instantly cooling. He was under the same sky somewhere, seeing more stars in it. She'd share her whole life with him under that sky, inky and vast, but always apart. Was he staring at the moon at the same time, asking the same questions? The flashing lights stayed in her vision, and pain stabbed her head. They walked up to the taxi rank and went home.

Paula was asleep when she got in, and Bea crept into her room. The dark of the city view from her window, twinkling lights masking the stars seeped into her cold and derelict mood. Bea turned from the world. The distance sprawled out, leaving her hollow. Kicking off her ankle boots, she let the sadness come.

Covering her mouth, her eyes burnt and throat closed. Stretched and taut, emotion clenched every muscle. Anger and bitterness, but mostly sadness pushed out her heart until it was nothing and spread thin. Bea curled up on the bed and wept. Loud and gross until her head pounded, and her mouth was too dry to swallow.

With her head throbbing, the migraine deepened, and she took her meds.

And it was done. Purged. Just the emptiness that he left behind. Bea took a slow, deep breath and passed out.

Clash

Bob barked at the wind.

Josh almost smiled as he dug the garden. The first signs of spring were already apparent. Snowdrops had faded, and daffodils were bright. Even the trees were in bud.

The ground was still a bit frozen, but he liked digging. He put some compost in the hole and set the cluster of bulbs around the base of the tree.

Behind him, he'd already got the kitchen garden underway and was just landscaping.

He stretched his back as the first spots of rain touched the air.

Squinting up at the sky, he thought about how tying up all the connections in his life left him isolated, and he needed Bea. God, he missed her. Her sweet laugh, her warmth, the passion of her.

Josh didn't love easily, but he loved hard. She'd shown him more about who he was than anything else. The memory of her touch and the sound of her voice still made his stomach dip when he thought about her. He missed her messages and their conversations deep into the night. The precious desire, and then the flood of physical touch.

It'd been too much too quick. That's why he resisted her so hard. He squinted up at the sky, though with a prudent eye, it had been best for him. Too late now, he thought. Too late.

It was worse than usual, though. Therapy had unearthed ugly things he needed to unpack, leaving the world cruel and unsettled. The perfection of their love stood in stark contrast.

Bracing his hands on his knees, his bottom lip trembled, but the pain wouldn't abate. The rain fell harder, soaked through his clothes, and ran cold along his skin.

He loved her so much and needed to hold her and take it all back, but that would never happen.

Straightening up, he tipped his head back as the wind got up, battering his face until he fought for breath.

Turning his head, tears streamed down his cheeks, and he clenched his body tight, unable to hold onto it anymore. He roared into the wind, screaming all the regret and hurt out. Not just for her, but his whole life; every hurt and anger, rejection and cruelty, the fear that ruled him in his youth and the fire. He covered his face to hide the tears and turned back to the house.

Trudging to the utility, Bob trotted alongside him, whining the whole time. Josh remembered the weight of Bea in his hold, the feel of her laughter within his arms. Her warmth and gentleness. Her love.

There was no let-up or escape.

Exhausted, he shrugged his things off, leaving them on the floor, towelled the dog, and went for a shower. He stood under the water until it ran cold.

Lying on the bed, spent and finally feeling nothing again, he went to sleep with his companion next to him, head nuzzled into his side as ever.

The sound of his phone brought him from an uncomfortable dream.

Josh put his hand out, squinting at the light from the screen, unable to think. "Yes?"

"It's Edie, she's taken bad." Sid's stout voice was muted with fear.

"Where?" Josh was already up, phone on speaker while he found clothes.

"Ambulance is here. Think it's her heart."

"Okay, I'll drive down."

Half-dressed, he put some food down for Bob, grabbed his essentials and headed out. They were carrying Edie out on the ambulance trolley from the cottage as he got out. Her eyes were closed, face dwarfed by the oxygen mask. She was so small.

He hugged Sid, who wiped his eyes. "You going with her?"

Sid nodded, locking up the house.

Josh followed the ambulance. The big hospital on the far side of the town made Josh shudder. All hospitals did, but it was his turn to endlessly wait about, and he fucking hated it. Edie was stable when they let them see her near lunch, and they'd barely spoken the whole time.

"She's stubborn. Won't slow down or owt."

"How long has it been bad?" Josh couldn't take his eyes off her sleeping form. She was iron and strength; a northern working-class toughness wrought through generations of women.

"A few years."

Josh turned to Sid. "You should've said, I'd have pushed harder to help."

"She doesn't want it. She wants you to go live your life, not spend it with us. We're old."

"You're my whole family. Not only do you deserve my care and respect for what you've done for me, but I love you. And apart from Barbara, I enjoy spending time with you."

Sid almost smiled.

"Things have to change."

"Aye."

He took Sid home that afternoon, and he saw to the animals while Sid packed a bag. She was awake when they got back. Groggy and quiet but awake. Sid bent down and kissed her papery cheek.

"Now, don't fuss me, I'm fine."

Josh held her hand, and she grinned.

∞ ∞ ∞

Bob ran from one end of the pasture to the other before flopping down on the damp grass with his tongue out and watched the chickens. Barbara strutted about. Josh thought it was almost provocative. He smiled and shook his head before sipping coffee. The sun was warm, but wind cool. Perfect. He took a deep breath.

Inside, they were cleaning and sorting out. The cottage had an annexe that'd been for Edie's mum, way back, she'd been a hundred and six when she died and scarier than Edie. Sid and Edie were moving into it so they didn't have to navigate the narrow stairs.

It'd become a store for nearly a decade, but it was cleared out and painted, ready for Edie to come home.

"There." Sid smoothed the bedspread down. He checked the time.

"Let's go get her."

Sid headed out beyond relieved.

Josh tried to persuade Edie to use the transport wheelchair the hospital provided for her when they got to the cottage, but she flat out refused.

Josh crossed his arms and stood in front of the open car door. "Edie, I don't insist on things often, but I'm going to. Sid has been beside himself with worry. I've never seen him like that, and you've scared us both. That means some changes need to happen. You'll use the chair. In the house, there's a walker. Use it. Do as you're told."

Edie pursed her wrinkled mouth and cut him a sour look. It softened. "Fine."

"Thank you." He kissed her cheek as he helped her up and into the chair, taking her into the cottage.

Sid settled her in, and Josh cooked in the cleaned-up kitchen. Things were going to have to change for all of them.

He thought about Bea. He'd nearly summoned the courage to contact her, but he couldn't leave Sid and Edie, not now.

A blister of pain took his breath, but before it set in, there was a squawking, barking, and a streak of feathers followed by Bob whizzed past the window.

"Not again."

Elastic

Ryan, the absolute shit, made her do one more stretch. "Come on."

Bea flopped back on the mat. Her legs ached and burnt. "Done." She caught her breath.

"Good. Hips are much more even. I'm really pleased, well done."

Bea didn't move.

"We'll do your review in two months. The hydro sessions and gym are still open to you. You need to keep up with the exercise you're doing to maintain, just like any kind of fitness. Use it or lose it, but it's whatever you need to do. Okay?"

"Thank you."

"Yeah, yeah." He tucked his hair behind his ear and grinned before helping her up. "How's Josh?"

"I don't know." Bea held her cane.

"I'm sorry."

"Thank you for everything." She couldn't look at him and said goodbye. After a shower and changing, she went to say hi to some of her old friends.

Charles spotted her and waved. "Well, you look great."

"Thank you." She had more volume but still got caught on hard consonants. It was easier to manage, though.

"How you doing?"

"I'll never go running, but who wants to do that? I'm okay." She stuttered half the words in a soft voice.

"Are you?"

"CAPTA can't fix everything."

"No. But we care. And there's always therapy."

"Thank you." She hugged him.

When Paula picked her up, Bea felt like she was sinking again.

"I'm worried about you," Paula said as she drove them home.

"I'm fine."

"Really? You need to decide what you want to do. Stay here, move away, I don't know. We don't need to stay in the secure flat, and it's getting cramped."

"Either nothing or something drastic. Maybe a short term let while we figure it out. Both of us."

"Good."

They scoured online for places in the afternoon, curled up on the settee with tea and biscuits when the court liaison officer called.

"Would you like to read an impact statement for the sentencing hearing?"

Did she? Bea glanced at her mum. She thought about her life before and after. She'd set into motion Mickey Bennet's downfall, and he sent a man to kill her. She couldn't even think about his name or face. She'd been asked this question and written it already. Now she had to decide if she wanted to submit it.

"Yes."

∞ ∞ ∞

Bea wore a pale blue shirt and navy trousers. Her hands shook as she clung to her cane in the waiting area. The new courthouse had light woodwork and green carpets. She stared at the pale walls. Both Selina and her mother were with her, but they were in the gallery already.

Her mouth was unnaturally dry. She'd tuned out of much of what she was supposed to do and merely went where prompted. Her action was in her choices, and she moved through the world like treacle, slow and disconnected from it. Time was odd to her, she was with Josh, but that was a thousand years ago yet just the other day. Bea was tired of her passive movement, pushed along by forces beyond her. She unclenched her jaw as her frustrated bent to grind her teeth gave her a headache. Her hands shook, and she opened and closed her fists.

It was nearly over, wasn't it? Perhaps then things might change.

Someone called her name. The liaison guided and spoke, but she couldn't take it in. It was a sombre room, the feel of it weighted and pensive.

The man was set back in the dock. Everyone else was quiet and serious. She steadied her breath as she stood in the witness stand, her weight on her cane.

The judge was an older woman, her grey hair visible under her wig. "Beatrice Golding, you have submitted your victim personal statement to the court and have been invited to read it."

Bea stuttered. "Yes, your Honour." Bea held the paper and took a deep breath. When her gaze was drawn up, Selina and her mum and even Matt were in the gallery. The one face she needed was absent. It still hurt. Maybe he didn't know. Why would he?

Refocusing, her voice was flat, but she projected as much as possible into the small mic. She focused on her breathing, her stutter making it tricky. Heat rose in her face. "My life was not exciting, but I was happy. When I started working at Grey's, I was saving for a holiday. Mr Bennet's statements on occasion caused me to go to the police. I thought I would be safe, but that was not true. I spent several weeks in hiding, terrified that Micky Bennet would find me.

"Then he did.

"There are no words to describe the terror I felt when the defendant ran me off the road. I received a serious head injury that left me in a coma for months. Not only did I have to learn to walk, speak, and undertake everyday tasks, I had to remember who I was. How to live in the world again. I live with permanent brain and nerve damage.

"I have adapted to my new physical self, but something has been taken from me. Who I was. My trust in any system. In people. Hope.

"I have taken back the things that matter to me, but I cannot drive, or work, or live without assistance from others.

"Added to this is the permanent psychological trauma," Bea's voice failed, and she stuttered and slurred. She took a moment, and the court was silent. "I have nightmares and PTSD. Those things will never leave me. They are part of me now, and the defendant did that to me. He caused that harm, and it will never be undone.

"He did it because I went to the police about his boss. It was cold and cruel. It was a transaction.

"I have no doubt he would have taken my life finally, if not for Joshua Cottrell." Bea's face contorted, and she covered her face. "Sorry."

"Well, thank you, Miss Golding. I have no questions. You may step down."

The court officer assisted her down the steps.

It was done.

Less than a month later, they were set to move into a bungalow. It was a new build out of the city centre of a mix of townhouses, apartments and bungalows. Pretty, quiet, and most importantly, two bedrooms.

Matt and Selina helped them move.

Bea was still reeling from the news they received. Micky Bennet received a total of thirty years for the accumulation of his crimes. The police officer got ten years, and the man who'd run her off the road got a minimum life sentence.

The weight of it hung over her, and even though it was done with, it didn't go away. She dreamt about it at night, she talked about it with her therapist, but she was going around in circles.

Nobody was coming for her. It was over.

"Come on." Her mum bustled past her.

Her room was small with a built-in wardrobe, and her bed took up most of the space.

The window faced the flat garden. It'd be nice to have a garden.

She made the bed.

All she could hope for was that it'd fade in time, but it was all tied up with Josh now, and she was pretty sure she'd never really get over him.

She curled up, checked her phone and missed his presence in her life; it was so empty without it. She scrolled the group posts, he shared photos of Bob in the garden in early spring bloom. She held her phone to her heart, fighting the pain of it.

There were no more tears to shed, but the ache remained.

"Bea?"

She sat up sluggishly.

Sel started helping her unpack. "You okay?"

"You've been great to us. I know it's your job, but I'm really grateful."

"No. It's not been my job for a long time. We're friends."

Bea held her knees, softness returning to her heart. "Friends."

"Speaking of which, do you want to come and be my date to a wedding?"

"Date?"

"Not romantically, I have a plus one. It's an evening do, not the wedding itself. The ceremony is private, but the reception is going to be massive."

"Who?"

"Stuart and Effie. He does our IT contract work, and he's such a sweetheart, though... stoic as fuck. I only met her twice at Denbridge get-togethers. Super adorable."

"Sure. I'd like that."

"Perfect."

The sheep with their new lambs dotted the hillside, munching on heather and lush grass beyond. Bob was obsessed with them, barked from the garden, looked back at Josh with his big puppy eyes, and wanted to go up the hill to sniff where they'd been.

"It's one night. Effie asked about you."

He smiled. She made time for everyone and was utterly charming. The last work party he went to, she'd found him hiding outside and talked at length about small village life and Chadford.

"Okay." He didn't want to go back. The temptation was so keen.

Bea was moving on. She didn't need him now because she had her mother and was safe. Her life was in Chadford. Not with him. He swept his hair out of his face when Matt ended the call.

He kept thinking about the idea of his guilt. He could apologise to her. To what end? She was better without him, but still. To be there. It was such a dangerous idea and made his skin heat. He needed to think about it.

Josh couldn't say he was a ruin in his heart. He felt... measured. He belonged in Deerbank with his family. There was peace in him he'd never known before. Therapy and distance from his old life had done that. He knew what was wrong with him now, but he couldn't have what he wanted.

His happiness wasn't quantifiable, and he wasn't sure if it was something available to him. Others could have it, be entitled to it, but him? He just wanted peace, and he was as close to that as he was ever going to get. Leaving to be with her would destroy it, but they had the memory of something perfect yet unfinished.

No, he'd not seek her out, no matter how he yearned for it.

Edie was sat by the open living room window. She had the view of the paddock and could watch the chickens from it. The fence came close to the window, just the side path between, and Barbara clucked and strutted close up. Edie used to knit but couldn't anymore, so she massaged her knuckles. The radio droned near her, and her eyes would drop every few minutes.

She was still fragile but getting stronger.

"I'm off."

"Oh, aye." She ran her hand over his and patted his scarred cheek. She'd only ever cried once that he'd ever seen when he was in hospital, and she came to see him for the first time. She'd never flinched, looked away or anything. One burst of angry tears in relief he lived or terror he might not. If she could bear the pain he'd endured, she would have.

Josh kissed her head, her soft greying hair washed and set. "Love you."

She frowned at him. "What is it?"

"Glad you're home."

"You're different."

"I'm getting there."

"It's not like you to go off to parties."

"No, but I owe Matt."

"Hmm." A devious light glittered in her eyes.

Josh headed off, and Sid waved. There wasn't much for him to do, and they could manage for a few days. With a resigned sigh, he drove out of the village and headed for the bypass. The closer south he went, the more uncomfortable he was. He was right, going back wasn't good for him.

Selina was in the flat when he got to Chadford, and it was a mess. "Hey."

He hugged her and then dropped his bag in the box room.

"So, I have a date for tonight." She had a wicked glint in her eyes.

"Oh. Anyone nice?"

She only smirked.

"Fine."

"Don't sulk."

He showered and napped after a snack. He rarely wore a suit but settled for a shirt and tie with a waistcoat. He thought it was a bit much, but Sel said dressy.

Leaving his hair down, swept over to one side, he drove to the banquet hall. It was on the river and a pretty spot. Very posh.

Josh spotted Selina's and Matt's cars but didn't get out. He stared at nothing and pretended she was there with him. He pulled at his collar, and with a grunt, made himself move.

Party

Spring was cool but beautiful. Yet Bea missed the cold and snow. When she closed her eyes, she saw white.

She clutched her dressing gown watching the birds hop on and off the fence from her bedroom window, surrounded by new growth.

"You're going to be late." Her mother brought her a cup of tea.

"Sorry. Yes."

Bea slipped on the slinky knee-length electric blue dress, which matched her cane. Checking herself in the mirror, she'd almost forgotten what she looked like dressed up. She lifted her straightened hair, the scar along her head hidden and faded, only a ridge as a reminder. She didn't mind it at all. It was almost like proof and a physical anchor to her life and experience.

As ever, it made her think of Josh. Everything did.

She set on her eye patch, not needing it as much was great, but it was a relief when she used it.

"A glamorous pirate." She shrugged.

The doorbell chimed, and she slipped into her pointy tan flats, grabbed her matching clutch, and headed out.

"Well, aren't you glam?" Sel wore immaculately tailored cream tuxedo trousers, white shirt and tie.

"Damn." Bea pointed at Sel.

"Ooh let me get a photo." Paula got her phone out and took individual and a few of them together. "Right. Have fun. I have a bottle of wine and Miss Marple to keep me company."

"Ooh, I love Miss Marple." Selina turned to Bea.

"This was your idea. Move it."

It was busy at the banquet hall by the river, and the Denbridge people were already there. Matt loomed large, front and centre of them, even though he was sitting.

"Bea. Nice to see you." With him was a beautiful woman with a pale rose complexion and large eyes, full-figured and shapely, she had a warm softness to her and held a cane. "This is Willow, my partner."

"Hi. Ooh, I love your cane." She sat forward.

"Thank you!" Bea handed it over when she sat, and Willow tried it out.

Matt was full of warmth. "We'll go and get one if you like." He was soft and careful with her but utterly relaxed. He went to fetch them drinks.

"Are you okay?" Sel asked.

"He scares the crap out of me." Bea watched Matt glide through the crowd.

"Aw no, he's a teddy bear." Sel winked at Willow.

"A scary bastard teddy bear."

Willow burst out laughing.

"Oh my god, I'm sorry."

"No, he has that energy, I get it. I was wary of him when we met. But he's wonderful. Takes very good care of me." She held a glow to her, a knowing light. Bea's heart pinched and took the champagne Matt offered her when he came back.

"Oh, there's Stuart. God, he looks pissed. I swear, I've never seen him laugh." Sel went up like a meerkat.

Bea took her cane back and followed.

Stuart was tall, tanned with short dark hair, glasses, and seemed uncomfortable. The bride, Effie, was so short Bea nearly missed her. She wore an ivory off the shoulder dress, corseted up the back with her thick, bright red hair was intricately wound and styled with flowers. She beamed, her pale, freckled skin almost luminous.

"Selina. I'm so thrilled you came."

"This is Bea."

"Oh my god, you're so pretty." She threw her arms out, shoes in one hand, and handed them to Stuart. He took them, expressionless.

Effie hugged Bea and Sel. "There's a buffet in about half an hour, but we're doing the cake first. It's all a bit of a blur. Do you want a drink? Stuart?"

He narrowed his eyes at his new wife and gave her back her shoes.

"Is he okay?" Sel watched him go.

"He's fine. This is his worst nightmare. I agreed to a small ceremony if I could have a big fuck off party." She laughed. "I love winding him up, but he's enjoying it, really." She smirked her pale skin flushing.

"Congratulations. You're radiant." Bea offered.

"Thank you so much. I've had too much champagne."

Stuart returned, held out the drinks, and then turned to Effie, more than a foot shorter than him. "Put your shoes on, wife."

Effie grinned, making her nose wrinkle. She slipped on one platformed high heel, then the other and grew five inches.

With a nod, Stuart took her hand. "Excuse us." He smiled curtly and pulled his wife along and outside. Effie laughed the whole time.

Sel tilted her head. "They're adorable, but you know, I don't want it. That life. One person. Just. No. I'm fine."

"I do. I want it. But."

Sel put her arm around Bea and was about to speak when S Club 7 came on. "Oh my god." She led Bea onto the dance floor, ditching the drinks, and they sang along to 'Reach' with a whole crowd, and Bea had no idea what was going on. Out of breath by the end, they were both laughing before re-joining the others, flopping down into the nearest seat.

A few minutes later, something drew her attention like a hot spot on her skin. She stood up, and her heart stopped. There was no music or chatter, just them. Josh in a suit, gorgeous and really there. She blinked hard, trying to make sure he was real this time. His lips parted, and sadness etched his face. Though his hair was down, he didn't hide his scars with it, and it fell in perfect thick waves to his shoulders. Seeing him wasn't like before when she imagined him, no, he was there and walking away.

She made a noise and stepped forward. Her step halted. "Why is he here?"

Sel didn't say anything.

"He didn't know I'd be here." She swallowed hard and went after him. It stung. It shouldn't, but it did.

The evening light had just failed, but it wasn't dark yet. The wind rustled and cooled the anxiety sweat on her skin. "Wait."

He stopped, and his shoulders slumped.

"How are you?"

Josh turned. Her heart hurt. All she wanted to do was hold him. "I'm fine. What are you doing here?"

"Sel's date."

He nodded and put his hands in his pockets. "I knew this was a bad idea."

She tried a few times to speak but caught on the words. She refocused her breathing and tried again. "Is it so terrible seeing me?"

He drew himself up and approached. "Terrible? No, not at all. Painful. I don't want to cause you harm any more than I already have."

They stared at each other for a minute, the seconds stretching out, the danger of the silence hovering in her mind until she couldn't stand it. "You look good."

"So do you."

"I miss you."

The pain on his face mirrored hers, and he lifted his face to the sky, taking a steady breath. "I miss you too."

"It's all over with, I'm safe."

"I heard. I'm really happy for you. You can move on." He pinned her with his gaze, shadowed in the gloaming.

For a second, she thought it was snowing. Gathering her courage, she took a step toward him. "Not from everything."

"Maybe you should."

"I don't want to."

"We don't always get what we want." His voice descended into a hoarse whisper.

"That sounds like a song."

He huffed a laugh and shook his head. "Bea."

"Right, yes, I know. I remember. I get it. Sorry." She tried to smile and be cool, but her eyes filled with tears anyway as she turned away from him.

Josh took her arm. "Wait," he said into her hair. "I do care about you, and my feelings haven't changed. It's not that I don't want you."

Bea twisted back to him, frustrated and sore in spirit. "But I'm not enough for you to take the risk. I got it. Maybe we're not right for each other then because I'd have risked everything for you." She searched his eyes before laughing. "Sorry. That was unfair. You gave me hope when I had none, and that'll have to be enough for me."

Hello My Darling

When he saw Selina's date moments ago, with perfect curves in a clingy electric blue dress, dark hair and a cane, Josh's heart stopped. Bea. It was too sudden, and he'd automatically turned to escape. There was no escaping. Hadn't he tried for weeks?

He caught his breath in the evening air as she stood in front of him. Sweet and gentle and so sad. Sweat had prickled when she followed him out, and it cooled in the wind in the seconds after. She was perfect. So beautiful. She'd put weight on, she had more colour, and she seemed stronger.

Bea was standing in front of him, baring her heart, fragile and yet...

As she turned, he couldn't let her go.

The sensation of her arm in his hold, her skin, vibrated against his. He'd almost forgotten the electric presence of being close to her.

When she laughed, tears slid down her cheeks. Josh couldn't help it, he stepped closer and wiped her cheek with his thumb.

Her words echoed in his thoughts. *You gave me hope when I had none.*

"Same."

"You seem well." Bea shifted her weight, and he led her to his car to lean on the bonnet, staring across to the river.

"I'm doing okay. In therapy. Edie's been really ill so I need to help more."

"I'm sorry, is she okay?"

"Bad heart. She's slowing down, but she's stubborn."

"How's Bob?"

"Brilliant. Runs about terrorising Barbara and eats everything. I love him. Cottage is nearly done." He turned to her. Her face was blank. "You?"

"I don't know. We're in a bungalow until we decide what we're going to do." She stuttered and fussed her cane.

"Do?"

"There's no reason to stay here. Mum's house sold. Her redundancy was great. We have no real ties to Brakton anymore. Just us. The insurance company are being pricks because of the court case, but Farroq, my solicitor, says it'll work out."

"You could go anywhere," he whispered.

"Yes."

The silence strung out as night fell. The sliver of the moon shone in the clear dark sky. Josh missed the stars when he was in Chadford, but he saw nothing else but her. The breeze ruffled her hair.

"You straightened it." He reached out and put a defiant wave into place, and she turned to him.

"I like the change." Her eyes, huge and beautiful brown and impossibly sad, pinned him in place.

Sliding his arm around her waist, he tried to calm his heart but let it riot and leant his forehead against hers.

Her voice was hoarse and quiet, and he barely heard her over the beat of music and hum of people at the party. "Don't tell me we can't have this. I know you will, I know, but please, I can't hear it yet. Not yet."

The tears in her voice nearly choked him. Pressing a soft kiss to her cheek, he moved closer to her mouth, unable to not kiss her. Her breath shuddered when he brushed his lips against hers, and her tongue gently met his.

Josh held her tight, one hand in her hair, the other pinning her body to his. It was a memory of the safest, happiest moment of his life. So right, and exactly what he wanted and needed. Bea.

She hummed and kissed him deeper, her need almost overwhelming him. He'd do anything she wanted of him.

They broke apart, panting, and she steadied herself against his chest. She searched his eyes, needing an answer.

"Spend the night with me."

Bea lowered her head and nodded. She didn't speak, but he helped her into the car and drove back to the flat.

It was tiny and bare, but the bed was comfortable. Bea went to the bathroom, and he texted Selina to say they were there. She told him where the stash of condoms was.

Bea came back in.

"Are you sure this is what you want?"

Bea set her cane against the wall and slipped off her shoes. Reaching under one arm, she slid down a zip and eased out of her dress. The whole time she didn't speak.

"Bea."

Stepping closer, in her pretty floral underwear, she leant down for a kiss, and he went with it, standing up and taking into his arms. The warmth of her body and touch of her skin made him hard. His dick ached for her, and the press of her belly against it did little to ease the want. Her fingers speared his hair, and he felt no unease, he loved the way she looked at him.

"Sit." She pushed him down when she broke away.

For a moment, he waited, the anticipation of touching her building in his pulse, and though their lips neared, making his heart thud, he obeyed.

"Once, we talked about different kinds of sex. Remember?"

"Yes."

"And all the things we'd like to try?"

He nodded. "You want to?"

"I do. Take off your clothes." Her tone was almost hard, commanding. He liked it.

Josh unbuttoned his waistcoat, standing, and slipped it off. He undid the tie and slowly unbuttoned the shirt.

He loved that she looked at him with lust and need. Bea wanted him as he was with no conditions. He slipped off his shoes, undid his trousers, took everything off, and held his head high. "I might need to just pop to the bathroom." His voice broke the tension, and she laughed. The most perfect sound. He pulled her close and kissed her, the ache in his dick deepening as the pressure built.

When he was ready, he found the condoms and a small bottle of lube. And some wipes. He took them.

She was lying on the bed, nude, perfect and beautiful, and she reached out for him.

Her hands wandered all over his body when he joined her, caressing muscle, scars, dick and balls, and for the first time in so long, he let someone take control of him. Not like when they'd been together before, but he allowed her to give by letting her take what she wanted.

A strange sensation, and for a moment, his mind wandered back to the hospital and the past. He stilled her.

"I'm sorry." She tilted her head. "What's wrong?"

He focused up at the ceiling, searching for the right words. "When I was in hospital, I had no control over anything."

"Okay." She sat up, tucking her hair behind her ears.

"I was catheterised. They gave enemas. I was tube fed. My body wasn't mine."

"I'm sorry. It was the same for me."

Josh faced her.

"When I woke from the coma, I had no control either. I was... handled by other people."

"You get it." He smiled softly. "I'm okay, but it's just that intimacy is weird, to a point, for me, and you're the first person I've ever wanted in my space. Emotionally or physically."

"Thank you for telling me. Your trust means a lot." She cupped his face, he kissed her fingers, and he needed her, desperate for the connection.

He held her hand, holding her gaze as he ran it over his body. Heat filled his lips and cock, need spiralling higher.

Her soft, dirty smile and big fathomless eyes filled with lust. He let her hand go, trusting in her as she went lower, and he spread his legs.

With a sweet kiss, she grasped his cock, teasing him until he moaned.

Playing with him, kissing and touching, lust sat heavy, and Josh arched up to her touch. Bea kissed down his chest, and he completely relaxed.

Shifting so she sat on a hip, legs curled up to the side, Bea faced away from him. Josh put his arm around her waist with her sat side-on. She grabbed the lube and warmed some, running her hand between his cheeks as she leant over, but her tongue teasing his dick took his focus until her finger played with his rim, her body half over him, elbows on his hips, keeping him in place.

Josh cried out, trying to keep breathing, letting her lead and willing to go with her. "Please."

Bea pressed in. His mouth stretched wide and squeezed his eyes shut. The strange intrusion took a second to settle, and she waited, pressing smoothly but slowly when he relaxed.

Letting his cock go, she adding more lube, making a mess, but the sharpness faded, and he shouted out when she found the spot.

He barely breathed, her finger massaging, and when her mouth descended back over his cock, he would've vaulted up, if not for the finger in his arse.

Squeezing her bottom, he cupped between her legs, found her pussy — she was soaked — and caressed all over, pressing two fingers inside. They moved in the same rhythm, and he needed to come so much, but he daren't move.

Pleasure hovered, building slowly, and not just in his cock, all through him; it was so intense, he shook, growling his breath. His thighs trembled, body rigid.

He needed more, and as she sucked tighter, working harder, he grasped her hair with his free hand, unable to do anything as she laughed. The sound hummed around his length, her tongue swirling, and his cries grew more desperate.

He twitched, unable to hold on, unable to let go. "Bea, I need to come." The rough need in his voice cut her laughter. "Please."

She moved her finger inside him more, and he spiralled higher as he tensed, the pressure in his body unbearable, and with a shuddering breath, he came in her mouth, watching her take everything through narrowed eyes. He lost control of his body with a rasping cry, hips jerking, and every nerve pinching.

Sated, he went limp, watching her still sucking and licking, moving slowly, bringing him down, and the perfect pleasure of her tongue and lips over his sensitive skin was unlike anything he'd known.

It became too much, and he stilled her shoulders. "My turn."

"I think you had your turn, you sexy fuck."

He laughed but hissed as she pulled her fingers out of his arse. She used cleansing wipes on him and her.

"That was incredible."

"Yeah?"

"Mmm." He rolled her onto her back and cupped her.

She relaxed under his touch, arching up. Grabbing the lube, he warmed some and massaged between her legs.

She gasped. The lube heated, and he didn't linger but worked up to her arse cheeks when she lifted her hips and then the tops of her thighs.

He held her tight with his free arm, face just below his, eyes holding as she twitched and squirmed, her cheeks flushed, and hardened nipples brushed his chest.

Josh shifted so he could kiss all around her breasts, and she trembled under his touch, their connection so intense, he felt her pleasure as she wound higher, arching to him, needy and grasping.

"Josh, please." She squirmed.

"Don't like it when you're under my control, do you?"

She writhed, almost sobbing, clutching his hair, crying louder as she came, riding his hand with the rush of her cum mixing with the lube while she panted and relaxed. Josh held her close, gathering her to his chest, pressing kisses to her hair. She buried her face into his neck and the moment was too perfect.

The words hovered on his tongue, and all he wanted was to keep her with him and tell her he loved her. To be with her was a dream he didn't know how to have.

Dawn

It wasn't dawn, but Bea couldn't sleep. She lay over Josh, circling a finger over his chest as he slept. She was calm, listening to his breath and heart.

But the bead of worry wouldn't leave her. It was temporary. He'd go home. They'd be apart again.

"Have you slept at all?" His voice was quiet and gravelly. Josh ran his fingers in her hair.

She loved that he was obsessed with it. Her small smile faded, and she kissed his pec. "A little."

"What's wrong?"

"What if we tried to be together."

"I can't leave them."

"I know. I could come to you."

"Move to Deerbank?"

She gathered her courage. "Here's the real question: not what you ought to do; not what you think is right; and not what you think is best for me. What are you prepared to do for the possibility of us? I'd never ask you to leave because it's important to you. I know. There is nothing for mum and me here. We've been trying to think of what we want. I want you. Mum always talked about living in the country."

"You'd move all the way there?"

"Yes. I've thought and fantasised about it, but if you're willing to see what might be, why the fuck not? Life is short and shit. You know I read out my victim statement? I hate that word. I'm not a victim. I survived. You survived. We both shouldn't be here, and we are. I don't want this regret for the rest of my life. I'm tired of this pain. I can live with the physical stuff, but this... this is killing me."

He kissed her. Hands everywhere, deep and hard, rolling her onto her back. Josh lifted up, bracing on his arms.

"Is that a yes?"

He frowned slightly in thought, chest almost heaving and his eyes alive. "Yes. You're right. Completely right." He cleared his throat. "We need to be sensible. Come stay for a few weeks, the both of you. See how it feels."

"Really?"

He nuzzled her face. "Yes. I hate being apart. It's horrible. You're right, we owe it to each other to try."

She grabbed a condom and slipped it on him. He cried out with a blissed-out smile when she put her hands on his cock, and he bit his lip, gazing down at her, taking her back to their first time.

"I want you." Bea squeezed his bottom, urging him inside her.

"Need you." He pressed in, filling her body exactly where she needed him.

They took a moment, breath mingling.

Josh kissed her. "I can still feel your finger in me." He thrust in deep, holding it and circling his hips.

"I can get a strap-on."

He went still. "Would you fuck me or be sweet?" He moved again, slow, aching need heightening with every deliberate movement.

"Sweet at first, then hard." Bea squeezed his arse harder, her fingertips pressing into his cheeks as she held them apart. "Like this? Arse in the air, or on your back, while I play with your cock at the same time."

"Bea, both, fuck." Josh took her, and she grinned.

She loved that the thought drove him wild, and her desire spurred his. He circled as he thrust, undulating into her, finding the place she needed. Bea raised her one leg higher, body tensing.

With her face buried in his neck, she came, digging her fingers into him as each beat of orgasm seemed to pitch higher and stronger until the pulsing release rushed through her nerves.

Josh stilled as she revelled in the lingering bliss, trembling, thrusting slowly, and kissing her.

Later, Bea cleaned up and wore his shirt. He brought tea and toast, and they enjoyed breakfast in bed.

"We should make a plan." She said, licking jam from her lip.

"Right." He stared at her mouth. "Um. I have to go home today. I'm taking Edie to a follow up at the hospital tomorrow."

"I'll talk to mum. Book the hotel. Maybe... Saturday?"

"That works."

She shifted around to him and cradled her mug close.

"What?"

"I can't believe it. I thought..." She focused on her drink, lightly steaming before taking a sip.

"I know. Relationships don't fix people, but we can help each other, be stronger together."

"We don't need fixing."

Josh nodded, frowning. "No, but we needed to be in the right place for this to work. I think I'm as close to ready as I can be."

He dropped her off a few hours later and kissed her in the car. Bea breathed him in deep. Holding tight. She didn't want to let him go.

"It's okay." He stroked her back.

"Is it? Tell me it is, tell me you want this."

Josh cupped her cheeks. "I can't promise it'll be easy. I'm still putting myself right. But I'm with you. I want this. You bring something out in me that I never thought possible. It's wild how you make me feel and want, and you're right. We should embrace that. I never really hoped."

"Now we can." Bea kissed his scarred cheek, and he nuzzled her.

She watched him drive away, terrified she'd not see him again, but it was going to be okay. It was.

Paula was sipping a coffee at the table by the front window. She silently got up and made Bea a drink, and they sat at the table together.

"That's the guy who brought you back, and I assume it's him you've been pining over."

Bea shifted awkwardly. "Yep."

Paula set her mouth and put her hands on the table. "When you were young, you were so wild. The boys you brought home." She smiled and shook her head. "But we got through it, and you changed. When all this started, I wondered how things would've been for you. I liked to imagine you'd meet a decent person who'd treat you well and could really love. Maybe you've found that because of this, but don't think I'm going to let you make yourself unhappy with a wastrel who'll twirl you. I'm not having it."

Bea ran one hand over the back of the other, almost smiling at her mum's protectiveness. "Fair but unnecessary. We've not talked that much about Josh, but I think things might be different." Bea cleared her throat before sipping her coffee. "Neither of us expected to have a relationship, and it was safe-ish because it was distant. That day, when I left, I don't know what came over me. I was so afraid for you and everyone I cared about. They tracked me, and I thought maybe by phone. All I thought was, I needed to get away from anyone at risk. Didn't think anyone knew about Josh. I didn't think, just acted."

Paula frowned, concern etching her eyes. "Is that what it was like? We never really talked about it. All I felt was this horrible terror. Farooq gave me scant updates. Not knowing was terrifying."

"I never felt anything. I was terrified but didn't feel it. I became focused. I had cash, ID, a car. It was enough. I did casual work, cash in hand. Move on, move on. All I wanted to do was come home." Bea took off her eye patch and wiped her eyes.

Paula reached over and held her hand.

"So when I saw I was being followed again, it came back instantly. I can't even think about bringing that to you. Josh... it was his job, it wasn't what drew me to him, it was his kindness and support, but he could help me."

"And now?"

"He said he wasn't in a place to have a relationship. I didn't like it but understood. He was at the wedding, and we talked. You have no thoughts about what you want to do, right?"

"No. I thought maybe the coast or countryside. A small life. Quiet. Maybe a little job. We don't need much. Do you want to go to him?"

"Yes, but both of us. He lives in this lovely village. All hilly, sheep, deer, a nice pub. Rural, but there's a town nearby. We could go and stay up there for a few weeks. See what we think of it, and Josh and I can date. Maybe. What do you think?"

"It's a big decision, and if you two care about each other, it's as good a place as any to try. We'll go." Paula frowned.

"Are you sure?"

"You know I'm not exciting, and always liked the idea of leaving Brakton. It was never good for either of us. We have no one. Perhaps this could be a fresh start for us both. I certainly don't want a city life."

"Me either."

"One more thing, I do hope you're being careful. It's a bit soon for babies."

Bea nearly choked on her coffee before nodding with a flushed face.

Ding Dong

Selina picked Bea up a few days later. "What exactly are we doing because it's not a swim session day?"

"Sorry I lied, mum was there when you called. I need a favour." Bea wore sunglasses, and it was a surprisingly warm day. "It's kind of awkward."

"Oh, do tell. Josh was very fucking happy with himself before he went home."

Bea blushed. "Yes, well, I need to go to um, well." She cleared her throat.

"Spill, I don't care."

"So I could've ordered one online, but mum might see it and ask what it is. Anyway, there's an adult shop somewhere nearby."

Sel grinned before laughing. "What delicious dirtiness are we indulging in?"

"I don't want to say."

"Protecting Josh?"

Bea faced forward as they drove through the town.

"I can be tactful. I won't say anything to him. Seriously, I'm really happy for you two. Like, it's so great. You both deserve to be happy. I swear I'll keep whatever it is a secret to my grave. I won't even take this piss out of him."

Bea covered her mouth, trying not to laugh. "Thank you."

The shop was bigger than she expected, and though she was afraid it'd be full of creepy old men, it wasn't at all.

Sel waved at the person behind the counter. "Hey, Tabbie."

"You know her?"

"She's a twat but runs the shop and thinks she's the dog's bollocks. She's not," Sel muttered. Bea found what she wanted. A display of strap-ons.

"No way."

"Sel, please. You promised."

"It's hot. You know. He's all beefy, growly masculinity. So I'm saying it, that shit is hot."

"It is." Bea scanned the wall of dildos.

"Can I help?" Tabbie came over.

"I need something easy to get on and off and comfortable. My left side doesn't have full mobility."

"Well," said Tabbie, scanning the display, "this is a completely adjustable harness with slip buckles and offers the wearer to have a double-ended dildo. It comes with six attachments. The dildo attachment pad is also moveable. The most adaptable one we have. It's pricier than the others, but it's basically a four in one type strap-on. And you can wear the harness, put one strap around the thigh with the dildo attachment pad there, and have it as a thigh strap-on. It's really amazing and super comfortable. There's a demo video online, but it comes with instructions."

Bea examined it. The straps were soft lines, wide and thick. She tied the slip buckles, finding them easy. The dildo pad had a hole, and the attachments varied in size and style. She liked the idea of a double-ended one.

"How would the double work?"

Tabbie shifted the attachment pad, which was a ridged metal ring with a stiff leather support. "It looks weird, but you insert it and slide it through the hole, and it sits low. You'll see what I mean, here." She grabbed the shop tablet and showed Bea the demo illustration.

Looked perfect. "Sold."

“Excellent.”

They milled about while Tabbie found a boxed one from the back of the shop, and they stocked up on a few things. Bea couldn’t wait to try it.

∞ ∞ ∞

The traffic crawled forward. Bea propped her bare feet on the dash and ate a chocolate before passing Paula one.

“This is a sign.” Bea huffed. She hated long car journeys. Short ones were fine, but as time crawled around, her thoughts interceded. The sound of crunching metal, screeching tires...

“It’s a test.” Paula edged forward.

The travel news came on announcing long delays due to an accident. She shuddered inwardly, pushing against the falling sensation in her body. She centred herself and closed her eyes. The seatbelt holding her safe. Her mum’s perfume, one of comfort and home, the radio station cutting over the sound of the wheels on tarmac and engine propelling them forward.

Bea opened her eyes as she stared out the car door window, and a big SUV was beside them. The electric fear pulsed in her, but a woman was driving, her children in the back. She wondered if those feelings would ever go. Possibly not, but she was working on dealing with them better.

Nothing was going to happen to her. Nothing was going to happen. The only horror left to come for her was in her own mind. It wasn’t one to battle or fight. It was one to soothe and forgive.

Her heart started to slow, and she shifted to ease the heat on her back before pulling out her phone and texting Josh. *Stuck in traffic on the motorway x*

Don’t worry, we’ll wait xx

Bea's belly dipped, butterflies turning all through her. It was sunny and warm, the green fields of crops already high surrounded them, and other than for the cars, she was so happy. Her thoughts turned to the past, of that day when her life changed, of expecting death and feeling nothing but a chemical high before she passed out.

Bea anchored her breathing. Trees rolled past, and the blue sky was stationary. Birds flew overhead. All that fear and uncertainty and stress lingered. It was so hard to put that away. Therapy helped, and leaving CAPTA was her only regret, other than Selina. She'd become really important.

Josh said the hospital was okay, and the therapist he used was good. There was a nice big leisure centre with decent facilities she could use. Bea had the tools now. It was time to use them.

Bea nodded off and dreamt of snow and Josh's arms around her.

A sudden movement startled her awake, but it was only her mum changing lanes as she headed off the motorway, and the traffic suddenly eased. They navigated the A-roads and onto narrower B-roads, winding up through hills and valleys, until catching the view, Paula pulled over into a layby.

They got out, stretching. Cool wind caressed them under a clear blue sky, the patchwork of farms and countryside went on forever with only small signs of life interrupting it. Paula took a photo of the view, and they were both quiet, leaning against the car, being whipped by the wind.

"Ready?" Paula asked.

"Ready." Bea grinned, smoothing her hair before they went on.

Bea's excited nerves wound higher as they followed the sat-nav's calm voice. The pub was just opening when they entered the village, and they booked in. She was in the same room. As Paula settled in, Bea texted Josh to tell them they'd arrived. She freshened up and rushed to open the door at a knock, finding Josh standing there.

"You're here."

Her chin wobbled, and she covered her face.

"Hey, it's okay." Josh embraced her in a tight hug with one hand in her hair, completely enveloped in his arms as he rocked her side to side.

"I wish it'd been like this the first time."

He held her face and kissed her.

Paula opened her door, and they moved apart. "Hello. I'm Paula."

"Hi. Josh." He cleared his throat. "Lunch?"

Paula smothered a laugh and grabbed her bag. The pub was newly refurbished and did good food, so Josh said.

The three sat down.

"What else is here?" Paula asked as they decided what to order.

"There's the shop and post office. Though I don't know how long it'll be open."

"Why?"

"Mary, who runs it, is retiring. Her husband passed, and she's not got the heart for it now."

Paula narrowed her eyes and turned her wine glass.

"You interested?"

She blinked, coming out of her thoughts. "I don't know. I was a retail manager for a long time."

Josh and Bea glanced at each other.

They talked the afternoon away until Bea's eyes dropped.

Paula cleared her throat. "Why don't you two spend some time together. I'll take a walk later."

Josh helped Bea grab her bag from her room, and he took her up to the cottage.

Bob wagged and whined when she arrived and sat on the floor with him, giving him all the fuss he could stand.

"Bea, do you want to rest?" She caught a hint of nerves in his gruff but soft voice, though his eyes were full of warmth and love as he gazed down at the two. Bob's tail thumped on the tiles.

"Only if you cuddle me."

He tried to hide his smile as he helped her up and then into his arms, carrying her to bed.

She clung to him, breathing in the scent of his skin. He didn't put her down but kissed her gently, lips hovering close in the quiet second after.

Bob jumped on the bed, and Josh sighed, setting her next to him before closing the curtains. He took her shoes off, and she slipped off her maxi skirt and crop top.

He stared at her, pulled off his long-sleeved top and unbuttoned his jeans. Bea stared, loving the way he moved, showing her his body, wanting him.

Josh slipped in next to her, slid his hand over her belly and dotted light kisses to her shoulder.

"Close your eyes. I've got you."

Bea nestled into his chest, her face against his heart, and she listened to it. He ran his thumb over her arm absently. She closed her eyes and relaxed. Truly let go. All her stress melted. No breath behind her, no fear, just them in the moment.

They didn't sleep, only lay there, everything unsaid and uncertain. Josh's throat bobbed in a swallow before he sighed.

"Okay?"

"You really want to do this? This is what you actually choose?"

Bea shifted out of her very comfortable snuggle so she could face him. "I never had direction. I drifted from job to job, thing to thing. Guy to guy. I hung out on the kink scene, thinking maybe it was something to belong to, but I didn't. I was okay at things but never excelled. I never cared to. I only ever wanted to," she frowned and sought the words, "not hurt people and be part of something. It's even more pronounced now; the lack of purpose.

I've wanted to fall in love, to be someone's, and I have. Why wouldn't I fight for it if there's the possibility that it could be ours? But. You have to be on board properly, not because I want it, but that you do too. No half measures. I know you haven't wanted this, and I get it." Her voice was clear and stuttered.

Josh didn't say anything for a minute, and the fear in her throat spread down her spine. She couldn't look at him.

"I was afraid, and I think being as afraid as I was, told me I wasn't ready. Instinct comes from self-awareness and experience. My instinct told me it wasn't time, but not because I doubted you or how I felt about you. That's never been the question." He kissed her forehead and stroked the back of her arm. "When I took you back to Chadford, I told you I loved you. I've never said that to anyone. You said you weren't enough, but you got it wrong. I wasn't enough. I had to work through it." His voice trembled into a raspy whisper.

Bea held him tight, her emotion bubbling over.

"I've been miserable and just... desolate. This weight in my heart for you," he dug his fingers into her, squeezing, as his breath hitched, "I can only bear it with you."

She sobbed. He sobbed. Bob whined and nuzzled them both as they fussed him.

Josh cleared his throat, wiping his eyes. "Tea?"

"Please." She kissed him, eyes shining.

He was so beautiful with his raw, gentle heart exposed to her. She knew how privileged she was to hold it.

Heat in the Light

Bea came out of the bathroom and found Josh with a tray of food and her bag. He was trying to convince Bob to go out and strode to her when he shut the door.

"I really need you." He kissed her, all tongue and need, he nipped her skin as he worked down her neck.

"Yes, I want you." Her eyes fluttered, desperate for his connection.

He made a strangled noise when she squeezed his bum.

"What do you want?"

"Everything. To be inside you," he growled through his teeth before kissing down, pulling her bra strap with it and sucking her nipple until she squirmed away.

Bea leant back as he held her flush against him and gently took his head in her hands. "I want to be inside you too."

Josh went still, letting go slowly, and smirked. "And how are we to accomplish such a thing?"

Her eyes darted to the bag. "Think of it as a reunion celebration."

Josh laughed, red touching his cheek, but he nodded. "You got one?"

"I did."

"I need you inside me." Josh kissed down her body, getting her naked.

Bea moaned and pushed him off, reaching over the side of the bed to open her bag.

Josh grabbed her hips. "Bea, fuck I missed this sight. You have freckle right here," he whispered against her skin and kissed the spot at the very top of her thigh, under the crease of her arse.

She fell forward, gripping her bag as he sucked her skin. Pulling herself together with a laugh, she unzipped her tote and pulled out the lube and strap-on.

The sucking and kissing stopped. "Oh my god."

Bea rolled onto the bed. "Not quite."

He didn't take his eyes off it. He knelt and picked up the tangle of straps, tilting his head to the side.

"Are you sure?" she asked.

He put it down, cleared his throat, and slipped off the bed. "I'm going to the bathroom."

Bea put the attachments out for him to choose, suddenly nervous.

He came back nude, and vulnerable uncertainty etched his every movement. He was so beautiful. His body and heart. Her skin prickled with the breadth of her feeling.

She smiled, wide and loving. "Come, help me." Bea stood. "Pick. It's your choice." She kissed his neck, pressing into the uneven skin she loved so much.

He examined each attachment and chose the double-ended one. He helped her wrap and secure the straps and went to his knees. Both their fingers trembled and brushed as they worked in breathy silence.

"Bea, you're so wet."

"Taste me." Her heart thumped and skin goosed. She remembered the rush of control and power of it.

Josh didn't break eye contact, clutching the tangle of straps, and rested his face against her thigh before kissing along her skin to her heat and slipped his tongue out to taste her.

Bea caressed the back of his head, spearing his hair. His soft licks and nuzzles sent shocks of pleasure through her, and with a hiss, she pulled away. "Put it in me."

She bit her bottom lip, centring herself. Josh didn't wipe his mouth, but heavy-lidded, teased the long thick length inside her; it bulbed out in a curve to keep in place. The smaller curved end stuck out, and she secured it with the attachment pad, the ring clicking onto it, and Josh secured the straps under her bottom and the tops of the thighs. It wasn't going anywhere.

He knelt back and stared. "Fuck."

Bea shuddered a breath. The press of the harness against her skin, the protruding blue dick and the thickness inside nearly overwhelmed her. She moaned, head falling back, hands on his shoulders, and almost too aroused.

Josh held her waist to keep her steady. Neither spoke but stared at each other. She tucked his hair behind his ear, running her fingers through the length, and was unable to keep her emotion in check, hands shaking.

"You want it off?" he whispered.

She shook her head, making tears fall. "It feels perfect."

"You are perfect, my Goddess." His dick twitched, precum already seeping out.

His mouth hovered close to the dildo, and he focused on it.

"Suck it."

"Suck it?" He smirked, but hesitated, licked his lips, and then sank his mouth over it.

"Good boy."

Heat went to every part of her.

"Will that give you a new appreciation for blow jobs?"

Josh narrowed his eyes and took it all the way in, and moved hard and quick.

"Is that how you like it?"

He hummed. The slight movement nudged the part inside her. Bea stilled him and pushed him back.

They lay on the bed, shuffling to sixty-nine, she took him as deep as possible, making him cry out.

"Show me."

"Oh fuck, Bea."

"We will."

When he went fast, and so did she. He slowed down until they found a deep rhythm in sync, but it wasn't enough.

He pinned her against him, hips moving in time with her mouth until they were all lips and tongue and the sound of humming.

Josh let the dildo pop out of his mouth. "Stop. I need to come."

She sucked hard and deep a few more times, pushing him to the point of no return and let him go, hand around the base of his shaft, making him thrust up. Bea incrementally squeezed, and he shouted. He panted and moaned, his face pained and desperate. She kissed the inside of his thighs and worked up his body, the strap-on brushing between them. She pulled away and grabbed the lube.

"Ready?"

He nodded, utterly desperate.

She lubed the dildo and put a healthy, cool dollop of it right on his arse and teased the end in.

He shifted and settled, taking a deep breath and nodded.

She slid in, not all the way, but slowly, easing past his resistance, and they both cried out at it.

"Talk to me." She braced over him, and he lifted his knees higher.

Josh grinned and speared her hair with his fingers. "I love your hair."

"I noticed."

"I love you."

"I noticed that too."

He laughed, but she kissed him.

"I love you so much." She leant up to ease the awkward hunch of her back, and he relaxed.

He guided her hips to the right angle and then let her work him. Her muscles strained, and he palmed her tits, pinched her nipples, and hissed when she went harder.

"Yes?"

"Please." He arched his head back. Hair streaming all around him. He was gorgeous. "There, don't stop." He gripped the harness straps and helped her move with gritted and bared teeth.

She grabbed his cock, hand still slippy with lube, keeping herself propped up on her other arm.

"Oh fuck."

The length inside her pulled and nudged her g-spot, and her clit rubbed against the outer part. Pleasure hovered, spiking with an intensity she'd never experienced. She grunted, body strained and desperate with Josh supporting her weight and movement. She lost all coordination and sense, climbing higher, ecstasy exploding.

"Fuck, that's it, come in me," he rasped in desperation.

Her body shook and twitched, hips moving faster, relishing every response and sound he made and riding the waves of orgasm. Wetness spread between them, and she sweated, the contorting pleasure tingling all through her, releasing the ache in her. Stroking his length faster, she locked her sated gaze on his desperate one, and he followed; the drawn pinch of pleasure went from his face, through his body, tensed and shuddering until he came, cum coating her hand and chest and him.

She would have collapsed, but he held her.

"Off." He eased her out gingerly, and she rolled back, her body stiff and cramped. He undid the straps as fast as he could, pulled the dildo out, and cupped her face.

"Josh?" she slurred.

"I need to be in you."

Bea swallowed, grinning, and opened her legs.

"Sure?"

She urged him inside her, and he grunted and thrust into her with his still hard cock.

"Take it, take what you need," she whispered against this skin.

"I need you so much." He took her. Hard and fast, unrelenting, and she stayed with him.

"Come on, fuck me. Have what you missed."

Josh cried out as she grasped his hair. Her body giving wholly to him. The orgasm still tingled in the soles of her feet, and she relished him inside her.

Eventually, he shouted a hoarse cry and collapsed over her, pinning her with his weight. "Sorry," he mumbled into the pillow.

"Don't be sorry. It was perfect."

He chuckled breathlessly and leant up. "I didn't come again, but I didn't use a condom. Shit. Let's get cleaned up."

Bea tasted her mouth. "It's okay. I had an IUD put in at CAPTA. I'm parched."

He passed her a juice, and she chugged it. Sweat clung to her, and pain throbbed. It was completely worth it.

"Are you all right?"

Josh held worry in his eyes but smiled as he cupped her face. "I think I might feel that for a few days, but it was... incredible. I felt it in my spine and scalp. Fuck, it was..." He kissed her. "You?"

"I hurt."

"My love." He nuzzled her. "I want to tend to you."

Josh cared for her. He helped her up and into the bathroom, tying her hair back before setting her under the hot cascade of the shower. He washed her with reverence and quiet. She relished his care of her and the love in it. She wanted to cry. There was nothing she'd hold back from him. Bea was revealed and uncovered. In a brilliant moment of understanding, she saw them with no secrets or mistruths; they were one, intertwined and undone.

He understood her in a way an abled person couldn't, and their shared reality bound them so tightly, there could be no other way for either of them. She could relax, and they didn't have to justify their physicality or explain it.

"What's wrong?" He massaged moisturiser onto them both but paid attention to her hip.

"Nothing, nothing at all. I'm happy." She moaned, relaxed at the bliss of his massage.

They curled up in bed, Bob allowed back in who sulked at the bottom of the bed, and they ate as the night deepened into dark.

Hearth

Josh put a shirt on, changed it, then changed back.

"Are you worried?" Bea finished doing her hair.

"Edie is kind of very northern. No fucking about."

"That's okay. They love you, and that's what matters."

They'd done nothing but fuck and touch and love all night, and he was knackered and yet never so alive. "Yes."

"What is it?"

"I have you for two whole weeks, but I don't know if it's enough."

"You have me for as long as you want me." She smoothed her hands down his shirt.

"Forever then?"

She laughed, slipping her arms around him. "Come on, we'll be late."

They drove down to the pub with Bob whining at being left behind.

They slipped into her room at the pub so she could change, and he sat on the bed. Bea texted her mum, who replied, saying she was just finishing getting ready.

Her things were dotted about, and he imagined them in his home, and it felt right. Natural. As it should be. She wore a silky gold tunic that hung lower at the back and skinny jeans. Not dressy, and yet everything she wore was beautiful to him, and the world around her in her physical space changed how he saw it. Something slotted into place as she moved about.

"You okay?"

He cleared his throat and blinked. "Yes."

"Josh?"

"Will you promise me something?"

"Depends what it is."

"If you don't love it here, will you say? I don't want you to feel any sense of obligation or... that you're settling. I need you to be happy."

"Being with you makes me happy. I'm mostly worried mum won't like it. What ifs are useless. Come on, I'm starving."

"Promise me."

"I promise. What's this about?" Bea took his hands in hers.

"Yesterday was profound." He tried to order his thoughts through their sudden riot.

"It was."

"No, I mean the connection for me every time we're intimate," his mouth opened, but the words wouldn't come.

Bea sat next to him. "Listen to me. You belong to me now. That's it. Done. And I am yours. Yes, I'm going to be a sensible bitch and not make rash choices, but I'm in."

They knocked on Paula's door, and Josh shifted with his hands in his pockets, trying not to look like he'd been shagging her daughter when Paula came out and headed over to the pub.

Edie wore lipstick. She only got that out at Christmas. She had more colour and had even put some weight on in the last few weeks. It was a relief. Sid stood, and everyone was introduced, and they ordered dinner.

"So. You're the one he's been moping over." She inspected Bea with her gaze narrowed. "Aye. Well, he's got good taste. I'll give him that." She winked.

Bea laughed with a blush. "It's nice to meet you both. Josh has told me so much about you." She struggled to get the words out.

Sid hugged her.

Josh kept glancing at Bea, happy and content. He knew then when she made her choice, he'd ask her to marry him. The idea he could have everything he wanted was unbelievable, yet it was on the brink of reality.

"I think I'd like to enquire about the shop." Paula sipped her white wine.

"Oh really?" Edie sipped her small sherry.

"I worked retail. It could work. I went down and spoke to her, actually. Didn't say anything about it, but I rather like the village, and we were thinking about moving to the area. It could be exactly what I want."

Josh dared a glance at Bea, who was fixed on her mum.

Edie leant in. "We fought for years to keep it open, but Mary can't keep it on. It's more than a shop, though. They have a book trolley library and public computer for internet access. The backroom is a community centre."

"What happens in there?" Bea asked.

"Ooh, let me think. Dance classes. There's the addiction support group. There's a counsellor come once a week. There's mommy and me, and yoga. There's even a mindfulness group with some hippy. Parties and the like. All sorts."

Paula, lost in thought, turned the glass on the coaster. "It'd be a lot of work. Early starts."

"There's a big apartment over it. Are you serious?" Edie squinted her wrinkled face. "Because sometimes people come into the village and get some romantic notion about village life and piss off again because the broadband is crap." She laughed and sipped her drink. She was much more herself again.

"I think I am. It was odd when I went in there, the whole place, really. Like coming home. I'm not afraid of hard work. It's all I've done. The only question is if I can manage it."

"Well, I'll say this for the place, we fought for it, and anyone who'd take it on, we'd support."

There was something warm on Paula's face, and she smiled. It was like hope.

∞ ∞ ∞

Bob tore along the hill trail. Josh held Bea's hand, leading her through the narrow way as she used her new sturdy walking cane. Cramp hit her on a steep section, and she halted.

"Too far?" Wind ruffled Josh's hair, and he swept it back with a smile.

"A bit." Bea caught her breath.

"Right." He picked her up, making her squeal with laughter, and carried them to a spot to rest with Bob barking in circles around them.

He set out their picnic and massaged the thigh for her. Bob lay near them with a chewy bone-shaped treat between his front paws, occasionally looking up and sniffing the air.

She lay back with the warm spring sun on her face.

"Bea."

"Hmm?"

The first two weeks had sped past. Paula had spent some time with Mary, figuring it all out. She needed to go and sort some things out in Chadford so Bea stayed. They had family dinners, and he showed them the town nearby, but every night she was in his bed. Their bed.

"We haven't talked about what we do next." He held his breath.

She patted the blanket, and he lay next to her. "Next?"

"Are you going back to Chadford? Do you want to move in with your mum or..." he went quiet.

"Or what?"

He laughed, shaking his head. "If I ask, there's the possibility of you saying no."

"Ask me."

"Or move in wi-"

"Yes."

"Just like that?"

She kissed him, coaxing him out of his thoughts. His desire grew into service of her, sweet, loving, and devoted. He serviced her until she'd come so many times she passed out. He loved it. His obsession with making her come was getting out of hand. He slipped his hand between her legs.

"You're not serious?"

"Please." He pulled her bottom lip into his mouth.

She glanced around.

"No one comes up here."

Unzipping her trousers, he slipped his cold hand into her heat, and she fell back. He kissed her neck, massaging a teasing finger at her entrance before slipping it in, using the heel of his hand on her clit. He knew every spot, everything she loved by studying how to pleasure and please her, just to feel that response, and see the ecstasy of her became his purpose.

Drawing a sharp breath, she arched up.

"That's it, come, let me feel it." He worked her harder, drawing her higher.

She trembled, tensing, the wet flood on his fingers, and clenching muscles followed until she slumped back. "Swine."

"I don't know what you mean." He pecked kisses to her cheek, bringing her down, and withdrew his fingers, sucking on them. He would try so much with her, fall into depravity in utter devotion and love. It was only her that could ever elicit such things from him. Discovering his limits with her was joyous.

She nestled into him, running her fingers under his t-shirt. “I’m going to move in. Then one day, you’ll ask me to marry you. I’ll say yes. Then we’ll go to the registry office. And that’ll be that.”

“Yes.”

Her hand stopped moving. “Did we just get engaged?”

“I think we did. But you know, we’re going to be sensible and wait for a bit.”

She squeezed him.

Lemonade

Bea woke, sweat pooling on her skin. She reached out in the pitch darkness and Josh's chest rose and fell in contented sleep. She steadied her breath, centring herself to him.

Her dreams had been worse during the last few weeks. She turned the ring on her finger and smiled. It was like it'd always been there.

Bob raised his head and whined.

"Come on," she whispered, grabbed her phone and went downstairs.

The ground source heating and the air pump kept the house moderately warm, and she had no idea when it started snowing. Thick flakes tumbled out of the sky, and she shook off the nightmare. She washed her face in the bathroom Josh put in that took a chunk out of the dining room — which was really a gym — but they could get to it from the utility.

She let the dog out, who trod the snow with caution, widdled and came back in, whining.

Bea fussed and fed Bob while making camomile tea and curled up with a book, but it didn't hold her, and the snow drew her attention. Memory flooded her as she absently turned her ring. Her life was good. She was happy and grateful for it. They spent Christmas with Paula and her new boyfriend, Des the postman, and Sid and Edie. They spent New Year in Chadford with their friends, and he'd laughed more than she'd ever known. It was a year since she first came to Deerbank.

The longer they were together, the easier he was. Therapy, work, and love helped him.

As weeks and then months passed, it wasn't coming so easy for her.

Bob climbed over onto her lap, not aware of how big he was, and they jostled for space. But he huffed his breath on her shoulder and rested his face against hers.

She rubbed the spot between his ears he loved so much.

"I hate waking without you." Josh appeared in just his bottoms, eyes catching the snow. "Another nightmare?" he asked when she didn't answer.

"I love you."

Josh frowned and crouched down in front of her. "I love you too. Want to talk?"

"I'm supposed to be working today." She helped her mum most mornings, but yesterday had been therapy, and she was still reeling.

"She'll understand." He smoothed her hair from her face.

"I want something nice."

"Distraction?"

"Please."

Josh smiled. A thing that came naturally now.

"Then let me help you." He lit the log fire, and the familiar scent caught the chilly air.

In silence, he grabbed cushions and blankets and shooed Bob out the way as he urged her to the fire. He ran his hands over her skin as he undressed her, stripping off himself.

She was sure of Josh though, he kept her grounded, her wild impulses abated in contentment, balanced in their play and communication. They were anchored so they could be free. She still suffered from migraines, bad dreams and paranoia. Her limp and speech didn't bother her, but the pain did. Yet she was safe and knew it. Without looking away from her, he opened her legs, and he settled between them, face nestled between her thighs, lazily kissing. His worship came easy in soft, easy sucks and licks of her clit. Instantly wet, she lifted her hips, using his face and holding him still. Her orgasm came deep and hard, her muscles tightened, and she spasmed as he held on.

Moaning, she flopped back, letting him go, and he hauled a breath. Josh eased straight in, mouth wet and hungry.

Their wedding had been sweet, quiet, and important. She wore her favourite summer dress with a bunch of wildflowers at the end of September when it was still warm, and yellow leaves crunched underfoot, even though flowers still bloomed, and they fucked for a week. The only people with them for the ceremony were Sid, Edie and Paula. Nice lunch afterwards. No party or fuss until New Year when they were front and centre to a massive blow out.

In the glowing light of the predawn, Josh made love to her. His quiet, gentle love brought her back to him, sliding in and out, holding her with complete devotion, and when she came again, she felt the snow patter onto her hot skin and saw flurries of stark white, prismed in pink light all about her. His hands and tongue reassured her, the cold nip of the air against the firelight became the memory of being trapped in a storm and was of another life. But she had this one, and Bea clung to it.

The End

Acknowledgements

I started Neon Hearts four years ago. It's existed in many forms, and this is its final one. Many people helped me get there. Sarah Smith, who reads my messy drafts and gives me joy. A beautiful human who makes me want to be a better person. My beta readers, Rebecca Chase, Bruno Céser Costa, Matt Hope, Heather Ann Lynn, Agata Veronika who's kindness and love for Bea and Josh warmed my heart, and Selina J who appears in this book and is the best side character evs. As ever, the Witlings on Twitter, the best safe place and sounding board, and the friends I hold dear, how could I procrastinate without you.

And to Ali Williams, my editor in chief, a clever, brilliant human who is open, kind and lovely.

Finally, for the last book in this series, I acknowledge myself. That I'm disabled and that's normal and okay. There is no shame to hold within that word. It does not hurt or harm me. It is an identity just like any other and I carry it with no strain in its weight. The people who showed me love and care who came with me on the real — and at times difficult — journey into embracing a new self, thank you.

It is not a linear path. Sometimes it sucks. Yet I'm here.

I am enough, and so are you.

Printed in Great Britain
by Amazon